What He
Would Not Do

~

Mr. Darcy's Tale Continues

P O Dixon

In dedication to my greatest inspiration...
you know who you are,
and to those of you, whose views,
helped to shape this tale.

Contents

Born of privilege,

his marriage, one of an unequal alliance,

this story explores what he would not do

for friendship,

for family,

for honour,

for love...

~ Chapter 1 ~
So Pleasing a Prospect

*W*hat *on earth was Elizabeth thinking?* Lady Ellen Matlock asked herself more than once that afternoon. The
frosty nip in the air made its presence known; taking its toll on
her Ladyship's patience, though certainly not her affection for
her eager niece. Even if setting protocol aside, surely common
sense dictated that the arriving guests be greeted initially inside
the warmth and comfort of the great manor house.

Whilst her Ladyship stood outdoors with her beloved
nephew and niece to await the onslaught of Darcy's in-laws, she
drew her arms tightly about herself to fend off the cold. Turning
about to direct her attention to the young couple, she quietly
observed Darcy and Elizabeth standing there, with their arms in-
tertwined in a loving embrace. The very sight of such tender affection cast a warm glow over her sentimental heart. She smiled
as she silently pondered, *is there anything that he would not do
for his lovely wife? Only time will tell...*

Just moments later, the thundering hooves of teams of
horses resonated harmoniously with the arrival of the many
fine carriages. *The shades of Pemberley—indeed!* Lady El-

len watched as tradesmen and their families, of various forms and fashion, descended from their carriages. They were to visit the entire month.

Mr. and Mrs. Gardiner, she had already met at the wedding that last summer. *Perhaps it is not so bad,* she contemplated. *If all of Elizabeth's family display any semblance of dignity as the Gardiners, this might be a tolerable experience after all.*

The four children who sprang from the carriage caused Lady Ellen to reconsider her stance. She quickly noted with some measure of comfort that the children were extremely well-groomed and well-mannered—*not too bad.*

The descent of Mr. and Mrs. Phillips from their carriage cast another cloud on her sentiments. There was no mistaking them. Their roots in trade could hardly be disguised, not that they felt any desire to try to do so. Lady Ellen thought to herself, *this must be the Meryton attorney and his wife.*

Mr. Thomas Eliot was next in alighting from the carriage. He quickly turned to hand down one of the most angelic creatures her Ladyship had yet to see, even with all of her years amongst the highest echelons of society. The young woman was by no means expensively attired. Her clothes were quite modest, but she possessed a beauty that required little embellishment. *Elizabeth's eldest sister,* Lady Ellen surmised. Indeed, it was Jane. The two little girls who followed her from the carriage were so adorable, that even Lady Ellen could not help but admire them.

A third carriage brought Mr. John Lovett and his wife Kitty forth. *Elizabeth's youngest sister, no doubt,* her Ladyship concluded, as she bore a remarkably strong resemblance. *Yet another tradesman,* she thought upon further perusal of Mr. Lovett. An even closer scrutiny of the general dishevel of the young couple's attire lent evidence as to why the two enjoyed the privacy of such a large carriage.

Finally, an occupier of the fourth carriage came into view. He appeared to be a man who was fairly aware of himself. Fastidious in his dress, the first thing he did was adjust his coat and straighten his cravat whilst straining his neck in a manner befitting a proud peacock. *Where have I seen that ridiculous man before?* She asked herself. A loud shrieking sound soon halted her recollection, as she observed what seemed to be some confusion as to who should be handed down next. The gentleman had reached for the eldest woman, but she insisted it was her privilege to be welcomed last—it seemed a grand gesture of sorts.

"But Mamma, it is right that you should descend first," Mrs. Mary Collins could be heard saying from inside the lush carriage.

"True, quite true, come along now, come along," Mr. Collins beseeched, hoping against all hope, to avoid a spectacle.

"Nonsense," Mrs. Bennet contended, "foolish child."

Some moments later, the confusion subsided. A young woman of a rather unprepossessing nature stepped down. By the time the self-proclaimed guest of honour got handed down from the carriage, Lady Ellen was beside herself with dismay.

What in the world has my poor nephew gotten himself into? What has he gotten the Fitzwilliam family into?

Her plastered-on smile no longer endured. She hardly knew what to do under such circumstances. The only comfort she took was in her opinion that Elizabeth might have been taken in at birth; that the woman before her was no indication of what her beloved nephew might look forward to in the long years to come.

Lady Ellen's hugely considerable distress was no match for her niece's tremendous enthusiasm. Elizabeth was utterly delighted. It was her first opportunity to see her family, since her marriage to Darcy. He followed through on his promise and received them all at Pemberley for December. He spared no cost in their conveyance.

Knowing full well, his aunt's opinion on greeting her family in the way they did, Elizabeth insisted that it would be no significant distress to her, if her Ladyship waited till everyone was properly settled within the manor, before making their acquaintance. It had been far too many months since she had seen any of her family. She was not inclined to delay their reunion a bit longer than required, simply for the sake of formality. They were her family. She had no intention, whatsoever, to stand on ceremony with them.

That was but one of several, of what had been, and what would always be, differences of opinion between the two strong-willed women. The first months of marriage persuaded Darcy not to take his aunt's side in any disagreement with his wife. He agreed to greet the arriving guests less formally, as well. Viewing herself as more than a mere guest in her nephew's home, but rather as a co-hostess, in a manner of speaking, Lady Ellen acquiesced.

Mrs. Reynolds, the Darcys' housekeeper, and her able-army of staff were able to accommodate the swarm of guests, and ensure that everyone was properly settled in no time at all.

All the women, having taken an adequate opportunity to make themselves more presentable after their long journey, assembled in the drawing-room to partake of afternoon tea and light refreshments. Elizabeth had her first opportunity to host such a large gathering as mistress of Pemberley. Much to her dismay, Mrs. Bennet was effusive in her praise of the size of the rooms, the fine furnishings, and the rich ornamentations. Elizabeth felt that some of her mother's extolling would have been better confined to silent musings. Regrettably, Mrs. Bennet was not one to keep her thoughts to herself.

"Pemberley is such a fine home. You were very clever indeed, to have landed such a rich husband, Lizzy." She traced her fingertips along the intricate pattern of the fine fabric of her chair and looked about the room proudly, "Though it was always my Jane, whom I thought of as the one to enjoy such riches. Alas, it was not to be, as Mr. Bingley never did return to Netherfield.

"A shame the place has not been let. I have encouraged Mr. Lovett and Kitty to make it their home. Not that they can afford it on their own, but Lizzy, perhaps you might aid them in that endeavour. I can only imagine what pin-money you must have. Why should your sister and her husband live in such a small place in Meryton, when Netherfield remains vacant? Lizzy, you must speak to Mr. Darcy."

Elizabeth knew her mother would be impolitic, but somehow she believed that, in Lady Ellen's presence, her mother's ridiculous manner might indeed be restrained. She was mindful that her Ladyship had made a concerted effort in accepting her as Darcy's wife. A fact that mattered to her greatly, as her opinion of Lady Ellen was as someone who upheld society's rigid views on the distinction of rank and privilege most decidedly. Any offence she might have suffered with the awareness that everything that her Ladyship did on her behalf, was done for the sake of her nephew, she chose to ignore.

All of Darcy's relatives, the notable exception being his aunt, Lady Catherine de Bourgh, made her feel a part of the family. How could she judge her Ladyship harshly in light of her seeming disdain of her family? Even Elizabeth could not deny the embarrassment she often suffered as a result of their antics. That being said, it was her family, and, therefore, her prerogative to be put off. Elizabeth felt as long as her Ladyship did nothing to show blatant contempt, or disrespect for her people, she would not be offended. Darcy revered Lady Ellen as a mother. She was, therefore, likened as a mother-in-law to Elizabeth. As such, she was worthy of her regard.

Lady Ellen was astonished by the words that gushed from Mrs. Bennet's mouth. It could be argued that she wanted her nephew to choose from the finest young ladies of the *ton* in selecting the mistress of Pemberley. Her years of unsuccessful matchmaking attempts bore that out. However, what she wanted most was that he should be happy. She had never known him to be happier than he was with Elizabeth. She felt the worst her nephew had done in marrying Elizabeth, was that he had married his sister's paid companion, his own former employee, and someone with a hint of family scandal in her past life. But a mercenary! She would never have ascribed that as Elizabeth's motive in marrying her beloved nephew.

Is it truly Mrs. Bennet's ardent belief that my nephew might purchase an estate for one of her daughters? For the second time, the only comfort she could find was in the notion that Elizabeth was taken in at birth. Even if that were the case, little good it would do the proud Fitzwilliam family. She was mortified by the prospect of what lay ahead if Elizabeth's Meryton family ever ventured forth in town and claimed an acquaintance. She had promised her nephew to support his choice of Elizabeth as his wife, and do all that she could in recommending her amongst the *ton.*

Would that even be possible now? She wondered. *With such a family as this, how on earth will I keep my promise to Fitzwilliam?*

~ ~ ~

With each passing day, Elizabeth's misery increased in having her mother's lack of common sense displayed so openly. Elizabeth thought it had been bad enough to have Lady Ellen as a guest for the past weeks, doing everything she could in helping her acclimate to her role as mistress of Pemberley, and more importantly, as the wife of Mr. Fitzwilliam Darcy and niece to the Earl of Matlock. At least she did not interfere with Elizabeth's management of the household. Mrs. Bennet's manner was another matter all together. She questioned every decision that Elizabeth made, with very little tact, and even in front of servants. On more than one occasion, Elizabeth found herself to be redirecting members of staff from one activity or another as a result of Mrs. Bennet's instructions. The most trying instances were those that involved Pemberley's renowned chef. Why Mrs. Bennet chose to interject her strong opinion in that regard, was hard to fathom. Nevertheless, she did and with some frequency. Her opinion of her second daughter being such that it was, she was far from persuaded that Elizabeth knew what she was about in her role as mistress of such a grand home. She was intent on teaching her all that she needed to learn.

The exceedingly unpleasant aspects of being under the same roof as her mother once again could only be made up for by the joy of being surrounded by others she held most dear to her heart. Nothing was more pleasing to Elizabeth than to have Jane with her at Pemberley. The fact that both were recent brides afforded what Elizabeth had hoped would be an even greater bond between them. Over the past months, Elizabeth was eager to share confidences with her in their frequent correspondence, much as she did with her newly wedded sister-in-law Lady Georgiana Middleton. Sadly, it was not quite as simple as she had wished. Elizabeth and Georgiana exchanged letters that spoke of joyfulness and uncertainties attributable to the first months of marriage. Jane's letters spoke of the responsibilities of motherhood and managing a household, and none of the less weighty concerns of young bridal insecurities.

Elizabeth missed her dearest sister exceedingly. She was extremely curious to know more of the man who married her sister and, therefore, was eager to spend time with all of Jane's new family. Mr. Eliot had proven to be an enigma to her during their brief association in Hertfordshire, the summer before. She was anxious to know how married life had affected him.

Thomas Eliot was a grave looking young man of eight and twenty, with an air of self-satisfaction and of little inclination to please or be pleased. He did not look upon Jane with the countenance of a recently married and overly besotted lover, but rather deferred to her, most significantly, as the mother of his children. Sarah and Beth, ages three and four respectively, were angelic little creatures whose delicate features brought to mind those of Jane. Whenever the four of them were together in the same room, it was always Jane, who interacted with the little darlings and satisfied the role of the doting parent. The girls loved Jane so much so that they preferred her above all others, including their nurse who had been with them since the death of their mother.

~ ~ ~

On a somewhat pleasant afternoon, Elizabeth and Jane leisurely strolled along one of Elizabeth's favourite paths. Elizabeth remarked upon the delightfulness of Jane's stepdaughters, a topic which Jane was always happy to discuss.

"Indeed, Sarah and Beth are a great blessing. They are divine. They so remind me of the children in my charge in Scotland, more so in countenance, mind you," Jane said, recalling her time as a governess and the often-times unruly behaviour of the children. "Though it has been a year since I have seen them, I remember them as if it was only yesterday. Indeed, my dearest Lizzy, it is the only one of the memories that I wish to recall of my life in Scotland."

"Dearest Jane, let us think no more of that part of our lives.

Are we not all blessed being here, together once again, each with our own charming prince to love and protect us? I daresay you seem happy. Are you indeed?"

"I am ever more inclined to agree with our dear departed friend Charlotte, in her opinion that happiness in marriage is entirely a matter of chance."

"I must say that I am not certain as to how to take what you have said. I know that our dear friend's view of marriage was rather pragmatic, and not at all romantic. I always feared you were settling for less in your decision to marry my brother. Can this be so?"

"He has provided me with two beautiful daughters. He is kind and considerate. Our home is quite lovely…, though nothing compared to Pemberley."

Elizabeth chose not to consider her sister's words as anything beyond sincerity, even as she wondered why Jane would say such a thing. She looked about her surroundings contentedly, still in awe of Pemberley's splendour.

"Indeed, Pemberley is lovely. To be mistress of such a place is more than I dared ever to have hoped for. However, I would be happy any place on earth as long as I am by William's side. He means everything to me, Jane."

"It is plain to see that you mean the world to him, as well. Is there anything that he would not do for you? Is there anything that he has not given you?" Jane asked, thinking of Elizabeth's elegant wardrobe, the many fine jewels, and the pampered lifestyle she lived as though she had not a care in the world.

"Jane, you are my dearest sister and my closest friend. Please do not think, for one moment, that I have anything that I am unwilling to share with you.

"Furthermore, I invite you and my brother to be our guests in town this Season. I am so looking forward to it, and I would wish for nothing more than to share it with you. Please say you will consider it."

"Lizzy, as much as I would love to take part in the Season with you, I do not know that it would even be practical."

"I only ask that you consider it. And do not be concerned with being practical, as you will be my guest; there is simply no cause for it."

"Indeed, I shall give it some thought," Jane promised.

Jane thought she had chosen the most advantageous option available to her in accepting Mr. Eliot's proposal of marriage. He owned a modest estate, comparable in every way to Long-bourn, her childhood home. He was a gentleman, but as with Jane, his mother's family also had roots firmly ensconced in trade. As it had been with the Bennet daughters, his daughters too, would have very small sums to offer in the way of dowries. For all intents and purposes, Jane's situation was as it had always been; whereas Elizabeth's was becoming increasingly entrenched in that of the highest order of society.

What might Mr. Eliot think of the prospect of being in town for the entire Season, when, in fact, his agreement to come to Pemberley had been reached with so little enthusiasm?

"You go ahead. I find myself in need of a quiet moment of solitude."

"Are you quite certain, Jane? Is everything all right?"

"Yes, dear Lizzy, I shall not be long." Elizabeth smiled and embraced her sister, before heading off along the path. Jane walked along in silent reflection. Elizabeth had given her much to consider. *What would it mean to have a Season in town? Surely there would be many private balls and elaborate gatherings.* Recollection of the last time she even danced pervaded her thoughts—the Netherfield Ball. The Bennet daughters had looked forward to that occasion for weeks.

Even the prospect of her wedding to Mr. Eliot did not offer such promise, as much hope. The lovely white gown she wore with considerable delight was the same that she wore on her wedding day. Despite her mother's protest, the wedding celebration was scant—it being Mr. Eliot's second marriage. Then too, Mr. Collins had to pay for not just one wedding—but two, with Kitty's nuptials following Jane's by a week.

Jane considered that her wardrobe comprised the same gowns as when she was a maiden. Mr. Eliot was as miserly as was Mr. Collins. Neither of the two young men ever wished to find himself in similar financial straits as Jane's father, the late Mr. Thomas Bennet. Jane, being a very sensible woman, understood both men in that. In fact, she appreciated their spendthrift ways. In light of Mr. Eliot's stern insistence that they should live below their means, Jane wondered if she stood a chance of persuading him to spend a Season in town, even if at the Darcys' largesse, where they would find themselves surrounded by the elites of the *ton*.

Jane sat down on a cold wrought iron bench. She smiled as she glanced about whilst admiring the magnificent wintertime topiary. With her arms wrapped tightly about her shoulders, as she reflected upon the many blessings in her sister's new life, she took time to consider her own; Beth and Sarah. It was not in Jane's nature to try to replace their birth mother. Though she barely knew the late Mrs. Eliot at all, she endeavoured to do all she could in seeing that the girls must always remember her. She loved her step-daughters dearly. Sadly, for Jane, in a week or so, they would be off to visit their grandparents in Lincolnshire. She could only imagine the utter emptiness in the Eliot household that would ensue.

Giving little to no thought at all to the passing time and increasingly frosty winter air, Jane continued to think long and hard on the many advantages and disadvantages of her sister's scheme. At length, she considered, *have I not sacrificed enough? Why then should I be denied so pleasing a prospect as the Season in town?*

~ *Chapter 2* ~
Two to Satisfy

F itzwilliam Darcy was no stranger to foolish people who had no awareness that they might be perceived as such. Through his privileged upbringing, he cultivated a higher tolerance for some, better than others. Those whom he considered his equal in consequence were more easily tolerated than those he did not. His aunt, Lady Catherine de Bourgh, served as the best example of that. Over the years, he had crafted a perfect prescription to deal with her Ladyship; a slight dose of reverence combined with an abundance of obliviousness. It did not take very long with his mother-in-law in his home, to realise that same formula might be equally effective with her.

He noticed that the great disdain she harboured for him during his stay in Hertfordshire was now replaced by a sense of awe. She only spoke directly to him, when it was in her power to grant him approbation or mark her deference for his opinion. Of course, he rarely spoke to her at all, if he could help it. That did not stop her from speaking nonsense to others in his presence. He was most particularly abhorred by her way of speaking to Elizabeth. There, he wished to intercede on his wife's behalf.

Indeed, they had agreed beforehand that Mrs. Bennet might certainly need handling during her stay. However, it was at Elizabeth's adamant insistence, that they agreed it was better that she would be the one to do it.

For the most part, Darcy was happy to see his beloved Elizabeth take so much pleasure in hosting her family, despite the strain it placed upon their personal relationship. They had gone from being inseparable to rarely having any time to themselves, overnight.

Three sisters, three brother-in-laws, two nieces, four cousins, two aunts, two uncles and one mother had been there for nearly a week. And those were just *her* relatives! His own aunt had been a guest since the middle of November and as a result, the inherent clashes amongst guests of such disparate social classes. Soon, Colonel Richard Fitzwilliam would be joining them as well, to be followed by Darcy's uncle, Lord Matlock. Finally, his cousin and his cousin's wife, his sister and his sister's husband planned to arrive in time for Christmas.

All Darcy desired was to spend time alone with Elizabeth. His mask of indifference became his preferred ammo as the abundance of house guests began to take its toll on his spirits.

Things began quite well upon Elizabeth's family's arrival. It could be said by all that the erstwhile haughty and taciturn Mr. Darcy was far more accommodating and agreeable than anyone from Meryton had ever remembered him to be.

He welcomed Elizabeth's relatives with as much warmth as could be expected from someone who had spent his entire life with a disdain for those outside of his sphere. Towards the Gardiners, he was amiable and hospitable, as he was when they first visited Pemberley. He endeavoured to find some commonality with both Mr. Lovett and Mr. Eliot. Not an easy task to be sure. Darcy likened Mr. Lovett to a male version of his wife Kitty. Though easily impressed himself, he was hardly one to inspire a similar sentiment in others. All this, Darcy might have found bearable, if not for the fact that Mr. Lovett seemed to hold Mr. Collins in some esteem. Where went one; so went the other.

Proving to make matters worse, albeit always a mixture of pride and ludicrousness, the self-assuredness that Mr. Collins once seemed to possess as Master of Longbourn, had reverted back to foolishness along with a heightened air of self-import-ance—now the brother of Mr. Darcy of Pemberley, the nephew of his former patroness Lady Catherine de Bourgh. Both Darcy and Lady Ellen were the unfortunate recipients of every bit as much kowtowing as once bestowed to Lady Catherine.

At the other end of the spectrum, was Mr. Eliot, who much preferred the solitude of a good book to the company of others. He was contented to pass the bulk of his time in the library. In thinking of Mr. Eliot, Darcy's thoughts could not help but tend towards Jane. Darcy recalled his earliest opinion of Jane, espe-cially with regard to her smiles. The impression he had of her then was no longer befitting of her. She rarely bestowed her smiles outside the presence of her two daughters.

Was it the tragic loss of her father, her youngest sister, and subsequently, her childhood home that has altered her so? Per-haps it was the year spent in servitude, under what could not have possibly been the most ideal circumstances that led to this.

In light of those very unfortunate particulars, Darcy could well understand why she had married Mr. Eliot, who appeared to be a good man—even if a tad too taciturn and somewhat aloof. Far be it for Darcy to consider either of those traits as lacking. Indeed, to his way of thinking, Jane had made an excel-lent match.

Why then, did it bother him to see Jane so altered? *Would she have been happy with Charles Bingley?* Darcy asked himself. *Bingley, who fell in love with a different angel as often as the change in seasons; Bingley, who married one such angel within months of his departure from Hertfordshire.*

Darcy recalled Elizabeth's words to him that Jane had been in love with his friend. Her words alone failed to bring to bear the level of remorse he now suffered in witnessing the possible consequences of his actions some two years ago.

Was it my interference that led to this? He wondered. Very soon afterwards he surmised, *one will never know.* However, one thing was clear to him. Darcy would not venture to interfere in anyone else's life again. Well—certainly not if he could help it.

Having done all that he wished in establishing rapport with his sisters' husbands, Darcy's thoughts turned towards his cousin Richard's pending arrival. The two had not seen each other at all since the wedding; not that Darcy minded one bit. No one else mattered, when it was just Elizabeth and him. She had certainly supplanted Richard as his favourite person in the entire world. However, his cousin remained close after. Darcy looked forward to seeing his sister Georgiana, too, as he had not seen her since she left Pemberley with her new husband—but even Georgiana would be one more competitor for Elizabeth's attention. He had no doubt that his sister would seek to monopolise his dear wife's company, as she had done the last time she visited.

If anyone had told him that it would be as bad as it had become—that he might actually relish the time alone in his study, apart from his wife, he would not have believed it possible. In an occasional moment of solitude, even if for only an hour before dinner, Darcy sat comfortably at his desk recollecting the past Christmas; the pain he suffered in being apart from Elizabeth, the heartbreaking uncertainty he felt that she might not return to his home, and just what he would have done to keep her in his life if indeed it had come to that.

What a wonderfully blessed difference a year has made.

His thoughts tended swiftly to a lovely sunrise from the not too distant past, before the frostiness of autumn mornings in Derbyshire put a halt to such amorous escapades—before the arrival of Elizabeth's family.

There was a slight chill in the air. They seemed to relish in the tranquil setting, neither saying much but rather enjoying their surroundings. Early morning horseback rides had be-come one of their favourite pastimes.

They soon came upon what had been christened their fa-vourite spot in all of Pemberley Woods; the temple where he offered her his hand in marriage, and she joyfully accepted. After they dismounted their horses and allowed them to drink from the pond, Darcy and Elizabeth settled themselves nearby, under a large tree on an out-stretched blanket.

The site of the temple never failed to rouse his sensibilit-ies. The same could be said of Elizabeth. It was there that they shared their first true kiss, there that he cherished his first glimpse of her magnificence, and first proclaimed his undying love for her. It held magic of its own for the Darcys.

As he gently caressed the locks of her long dark hair, he said, "You have been very quiet this morning. Tell me, what is on your mind?"

"Oh—I was thinking of how much I love this place."

"Indeed, I have always loved it here and now even more so."

"Yes, this is our place."

"An enchanting place that is ours alone... I wish that it will always be so."

"How could I deny you anything that you might wish for?" She asked as she leaned towards Darcy to feather-light

kisses along his neckline. At length, Darcy teased her earlobe and sucked gently upon her neck.

"In that case, I wish for..., a repeat of last night."

"It is a bit too chilly for that. Perhaps we might try something different," she urged as she encouraged him to sit up and lean back against the giant tree. "Allow me," she said as she unfastened his flap, freeing him.

Then she slowly rose to her feet. "Of course, I will have to do without these," she teased as she stepped out of her unmentionables. Elizabeth eased herself upon Darcy's lap and wrapped her legs around his body. They connected with one another in an unhurried penetrating enfold and soon found relaxation in a comfortable and satisfying tantric embrace.

Darcy whispered, "Mrs. Darcy, I require these to be removed as well," as he removed her riding jacket, followed by her habit shirt, and then lowered her chemise fully. The effect of the crisp air was not surprising. He caressed and suckled her, as he lifted the blanket about her bare shoulders to shelter her from the early morning air. Deeply in love, both enjoyed the same harmonious rhythm. In seeking each other's eyes, the two shared a profoundly sensual yet spiritual connection.

Elizabeth whispered, "You must promise me that you will return to this moment when my family becomes too unbearable," she kissed his cheek softly, "promise me."

"I do—I promise I will do whatever I can in ensuring your happiness," he murmured, as he cherished her with his kiss and then drew her head to rest upon his shoulder.

~ ~ ~

Even with a house full of guests, most of whom now held little interest to him, Darcy was obliged to spend much time and energy entertaining them, and not enough time with estate business. Thank goodness for his steward. There were some matters that his steward did not address, specifically those that pertained to his dealings in town. Darcy sat in his study late one night to catch up on his correspondence. He came across an all too familiar handwriting on one particular letter. It was one he had not occasioned to lay eyes upon since the year before. He wondered why his solicitor had allowed it to be sent to his home. It regarded Madam Adele's establishment, the brothel that he had patronised often in his past and as recently as a year and a half ago.

After quickly perusing the contents of the letter, Darcy could draw only one conclusion. "Richard!" Darcy shouted out loud. *Am I expected to give financial support for his debauchery for the rest of our lives?* He asked himself, while thinking he could not wait to confront his cousin.

Never before had Darcy been opposed to the many calls on his purse by his cousin Richard, in order that they might enjoy a similar lifestyle. Neither cost, nor intent was of concern to Darcy. In certain respects, Richard had financial carte blanche. *Is there really any reason for that arrangement to change?* He wondered.

Upon Richard's arrival a couple of days later, the issue of how he chose to live his life was relegated to the back of Darcy's mind. Darcy had reached the point where he would only tolerate his guests at dinner and during the obligatory after dinner gathering in the drawing-room. The after dinner tradition when gentlemen would "pass the port" before joining the women was rushed or avoided all together as Darcy was most anxious to see an early end to each evening's entertainment. Mr. Collins's obsequiousness alone was enough to offset Mr. Gardiner's good sense and taste. Mrs. Bennet's foolishness and her harsh treatment of Elizabeth were increasingly abhorrent to him. Mrs. Phillips's vulgarity, he found deplorable.

Richard provided a lifeline of escape for Darcy. The two were always inseparable whenever Richard visited Pemberley before. That visit proved no different than any other. Elizabeth, on the other hand, was quite disconcerted. Now observing her husband, with the ingenious eye of a wife, Elizabeth could discern just how symbiotic the two men were. Lady Ellen often remarked that the two were as thick as thieves. Even Elizabeth had been critical of the two, as she was forced to recall, during her argument with Darcy on that fateful day in June. When she said they were 'two peas in a pod', she supposed she was angry and overly dramatic. She was obliged to consider the truth of her hastily spoken words.

In the beginning of her acquaintance with Richard, he was the one most eager to bestow his attentions upon her, and Darcy endeavoured to hide his regard. Elizabeth was, to a certain extent, distrustful of the former even then. She recalled Darcy once telling her that outside of Richard and Georgiana, she was the most significant person in the world to him, but that was in the earliest days of their friendship. *Just where do I now figure in his esteem?* She asked herself. *Am I to compete with Richard as most important, as it now seems?*

As she mulled it over more, it occurred to her that the two men behaved exactly as they had the summer before last when the Bingleys were guests at Pemberley. And yet, it had scarcely warranted her attention. Suddenly, it had come to vex her exceedingly. Richard assumed a somewhat proprietary attitude of the time spent with Darcy that even she, Mrs. Darcy herself, often felt like an intruder.

It had gone far enough, in Elizabeth's opinion. The night before, Elizabeth had waited up hours in their bed, perusing the pages of a fashion magazine that her aunt Gardiner brought from town. As much as she enjoyed spending time with her sister Jane, she had come to cherish her time alone with her husband. She was eager to share confidences she had gleaned from her many interactions with her family, as had become a delightful diversion betwixt the two of them. A house full of guests afforded so little time for the two of them simply to converse. She missed that.

She awoke that morning to find the fashion magazine on the bedside table. She did not recall placing it there. She surmised she had fallen asleep whilst waiting for her husband. Darcy's side of the bed showed evidence of him having slept there. As Elizabeth was not a late riser, she wondered where he might be at such an early hour.

Darcy did not even bother to make an appearance at breakfast. Elizabeth endeavoured to mask her displeasure in being completely unable to account for his absence amongst inquiring minds. She was not in the habit of checking up on her husband. His inattention to his responsibilities as host demanded that she do so that particular morning. Having summoned his valet, inquiring of Mr. Darcy's whereabouts, she avoided, as best she could, appearing too stern.

"Mr. Walters, thank you for your promptness. It seems my husband has gone missing. Are you aware of what time he left this morning, and more importantly, when he might return?"

Mr. Walters, being a most loyal employee, responded cautiously. "Yes, madam, Mr. Darcy informed me that Colonel Fitzwilliam and he planned an early morning hunting outing. He, however, gave no indication of when he might return." He hoped that would be the end of it. The last thing he wanted was Mrs. Darcy making a habit of asking him of his master's comings and goings. He knew more so than anyone, the influence that Colonel Fitzwilliam had on his master. He never wished to pry in Mr. Darcy's affairs; but the late nights spent in his cousin's company was nothing new, neither was the drinking. Evidently, that had not changed with his master's marriage. *What if nothing else has changed?* Mr. Walters asked himself.

Elizabeth interrupted his silent deliberation. "Again, I thank you. I want to be informed immediately upon Mr. Darcy's return. Will you see to that?"

"Yes, madam, is there anything else that you wish of me?"

"No, that is all for now. You may go."

~ ~ ~

Elizabeth stood poised just outside the closed-door of Darcy's private study. She did not wish to come across as too demanding or too chastising of her husband. He was master of Pemberley, she was mistress, and therein was a hierarchy that must be revered, even amongst close family members.

Elizabeth entered the room, intent upon discussing a matter of considerable importance to her. She was not surprised to see Richard was there. *Where else would he be?* She asked herself. When it became clear that all her more subtle attempts to send him on his way had failed, she asked Richard, in no uncertain terms, to excuse them. Richard looked at her oddly. He then looked to Darcy as if he meant to have Darcy insist that there was no need for privacy.

Darcy suddenly became deeply engrossed in some paperwork before him. Elizabeth was on her own. Richard was on his own. Darcy was not unaware of the escalating tension between his two favourite people—he simply had no interest in intervening, believing as he did that they would be able to work it out. Thinking to himself, *surely, Richard can see that he owes my wife the utmost deference. Surely, Elizabeth can see that Richard is a prick. Perhaps not...*

"Mrs. Darcy, I will be happy to see you in but a few moments. First, I must speak with Richard. I will meet you in your sitting-room."

Elizabeth could not believe it! Her husband dismissed *her*, not Richard. She would not allow either of the two men to know the true extent of her outrage.

"Very well, Mr. Darcy," she stated calmly, turned, and left the room, not bothering to close the door, for even the calmest demeanour would not have prevented its being slammed shut.

Darcy walked over to close the door and then returned to his large mahogany desk. "Richard, why on earth do you persist in vexing my wife?"

"Come now, Darcy, you must admit she handles it rather poorly, which only enhances her charms."

"Nevertheless, stop it! You are not endearing yourself to her at all you know. I think she dislikes you very much."

"I imagine I should be afraid," he said sarcastically.

"Just give it a rest!" Darcy barked impatiently, as he stood to leave the room.

When Darcy joined Elizabeth in her sitting-room, there was no mistaking; she was upset. The boyishly innocent smile that graced his countenance did nothing to dissuade her.

She began immediately. "Pray tell me, why my husband is never to be found during the day in the absence of Richard's company."

"Is that all you wished to discuss with me?" Darcy asked, clearly not taking the matter as seriously as she.

"When is he ever planning to leave?"

"I have no idea. Richard arranges his schedule for his own convenience."

"Perhaps you might plant the idea in his head, that it is time to be on his way."

"Why would I do that, Elizabeth?"

"Because—I wish it!"

"Elizabeth, I am here now. What is it that you wish to discuss? If it is my company that you wish for, let us remedy that immediately with no more talk of Richard."

Not at all pleased with his manner of sidestepping her request, she jested, "Are you absolutely certain that Richard will not miss your company too much? I have no wish to come between you two."

"You need not worry about that, my love," he said, as he pulled her from her seat into his arms and kissed her, adoringly along her neckline.

"This is not what I had in mind."

"What did you have in mind?"

"I miss you. I feel utterly alone when we are apart."

"We have a house full of guests. How can you possibly feel alone?"

"I want you by my side. Why am I expected to entertain so many on my own, while you remain cloistered with Richard?"

"You know that I detest performing to strangers," he said, while continuing his seductive tease.

"Strangers, Mr. Darcy? Is not my family, your family? How are they thus considered strangers?"

Bringing to mind Mr. Collins, Mrs. Phillips and Mrs. Bennet, he thought to himself, *they are by far, the strangest people whom I have ever met.* He said, "Please, Elizabeth."

"This is not open to debate. I expect you to spend as much time with my brothers as you do with your cousin. They should be made to feel as welcome as he."

"And of what benefit is that to me?"

"You sir, will benefit from the knowledge that you are satisfying your wife, at the same time as you are fulfilling your responsibilities as host to everyone."

"I can envision a number of other ways to satisfy my wife, none of which involve having to suffer spending time with those I would rather wish to avoid."

"It takes two to satisfy, dear husband."

"Shall we test that assertion, dear wife?"

"I would rather not. At the moment, I prefer to have you test your social skills; starting with Mr. Collins, whom I know to be looking forward to spending more time in gentlemanly pursuits—perhaps a horseback tour about the estate."

Whilst stoking mounting involuntary tremors of desire, and further frustrating her purpose in summoning him, Darcy continued to test his wife's claim that it took two to satisfy, and she persisted in having her own way. Finally, after managing the situation to secure Darcy's promise to do a better job in spending time with others besides Richard, they were free to spend some quality time with one another. As it turned out, both Darcys were absent from all their guests for the next hour or so.

~ ~ ~

Some of the Hertfordshire guests were not at liberty to remain at Pemberley for the entire month. the Phillipses proved to be particularly welcomed early departing guests, to Elizabeth and Darcy, to be sure and most especially to Lady Ellen. She was relieved that her husband had yet to arrive. Lord Matlock would be shocked to see just how deeply Elizabeth's family was rooted in trade. A less welcome departure was that of Mr. Eliot.

His daughters were to spend Christmas with their maternal grandparents, as had been their family's practice since the death of the young girls' mother. As the girls were their grandparents' only living relatives, Mr. Eliot was not inclined to disappoint them. He planned to convey his daughters to Lincolnshire and then return to his own home in Hertfordshire, for the rest of the year.

Jane was faced with a choice between remaining at Pemberley with her family, especially Elizabeth, and leaving with her husband. Now given a choice, one that had not been available to her before Elizabeth's invitation to town, a decision to forego the trip to her husband's former in-laws was easily made. They had not quite accepted Jane as a true member of their extended family, in spite of the children's adoration for their step-mother. Therefore, the scheme was settled. Jane would stay at Pemberley and return to town with the Darcys in January, where they would be joined by her husband. In truth, Jane was as keen as was Elizabeth to enjoy the upcoming Season.

In the days following Mr. Eliot's going, as disappointed as she was that he was no longer a member of their family party, Elizabeth should have been very pleased to see that Richard spent far less time monopolising her husband. She was not. It seemed that Darcy's loss had become her dear sister's gain. The attentions that Richard bestowed were most eagerly received by Jane. The two were becoming increasingly more comfortable in one another's company with each passing day.

In as much as she did not wish to confess it, as did her husband, Elizabeth too suspected somewhat of a change in her eldest sister; a bit of cynicism, she had never perceived. On more than one occasion, she hearkened back to Jane's words, or rather precisely those of the late Mrs. Collins. *Happiness in marriage is entirely a matter of chance.* Elizabeth supposed it might be so, especially as she studied the Eliot family closely. Though, they certainly had all the makings of happiness.

Dear Charlotte, how prescient and always ever so practical...how I miss her, Elizabeth reflected. Charlotte had been Elizabeth's closest friend, except Jane, for as long as she could remember. In a morbidly satirical change of destiny, the tragedy of her death during childbirth had been the means of restoring the Bennet family in their beloved home, Longbourn, with Mary's marriage to the desolate widower, Mr. Collins. As it invariably turned out, Elizabeth was scarcely able to think of her family's return to Longbourn without remembering the heart wrenching chain of events that led to their eviction in the first place. During such times, she suffered, once again, the loss of her dear father. Mr. Bennet had been killed whilst endeavouring unsuccessfully, to recover his youngest daughter. Miss Lydia Bennet was persuaded to run off with a man nearly twice her age, named Lieutenant Wickham. He was more than someone whom the Bennet family had learnt to trust; he, at one time, could be counted as a favourite of Elizabeth's. Both a scoundrel and a coward, he accidentally shot and killed the young girl, just before committing the final act of murder of the elderly gentleman, under the guise of self-defence.

Oh how the Bennet family had suffered! That was but one of the reasons, Elizabeth desperately wanted to believe there was the prospect of happiness in her sister's circumstances. The budding relationship with Colonel Fitzwilliam could not by any means be good; not according to Elizabeth's way of thinking.

~ *Chapter 3* ~
All That Entails

The third Wednesday occasioned the arrival of Lord and
Lady Harry Middleton. Theirs preceded Lord Matlock's
by one day, as he had been detained a bit longer than expected
on estate business. A further boon for Mr. Collins it was, to be
surrounded by even more illustrious party members. The next
day's arrival of Lady Ellen's eldest son, Lord Robert and his
wife, Lady Elise, proved more than overwhelming to him. There
were lords and ladies all about, and he was bound to pay each
of them some particular measure of deference and attention.

Mrs. Bennet, by then had ceased her foolish ramblings on
the stroke of luck of her daughter Lizzy, and the misfortune of
her eldest daughter Jane, that it had not been her instead. Even
she could not fail to see the deep displeasure it caused her son-
in-law whenever she carried on in that fashion. Furthermore, she
was not apt to continue to risk his benevolence—a notion suggested to her by none other than Lady Ellen.

In vain, her Ladyship spoke with Elizabeth of the outright
disrespect shown by her mother and how it might undermine
Elizabeth's standing amongst her staff. Though the staff de-

ferred to Elizabeth as a member of the family, even before her marriage to their master, they could not help but remember that just as they were, she had also been an employee in the household. Lady Ellen sensed, more than Elizabeth, how it might seem to the staff to see their mistress so little respected by her own mother. She prevailed upon Elizabeth to assert her authority over her mother, in her own household. When all else failed, Lady Ellen took Mrs. Bennet aside to explain the undesirable consequences of her actions, should she persist in her outrageous behaviour. A hollow threat, it might have been, but Mrs. Bennet could have no way of knowing for certain.

Finally, with everyone getting along swimmingly, personality clashes were few and far between. Georgiana was overjoyed to make Jane's acquaintance at last. Having heard so much about her from Elizabeth over the past couple of years, she felt as if they were intimate friends already. Georgiana's openness extended to Mary as well, much to Darcy's delight.

It turned out; Darcy had begun to notice a strange malady which began at the onset of his guests' arrival a few weeks prior. When he could, he would excuse himself from his guests for a few moments of solitude in his study, under the guise of tending to urgent estate matters. The splitting headaches would quickly subside. He could not help but credit his sufferings to his sister-in-law Mary, and her insistence upon exhibiting on the pianoforte each night after dinner. He found he always felt that way after listening to her play for any extended amount of time. He felt that if he had to spend one more evening listening to Mary perform on the pianoforte, he would destroy the grand instrument himself.

In a flash, Darcy knew what he must do. He knew exactly the right gift to bestow upon his new sister. Sitting comfortably at his desk, late one night, under the dim light of a single candle, he reached for his pen and paper and wrote to his solicitor in town.

Though Mary's proficiency on the instrument had improved considerably under Georgiana's tutelage, it was still not such that Darcy did not continue to suffer through her performances. While making his way to his study one evening, he reflected quietly upon his Christmas gift to his new sister; three months of training with a London master. He had contracted to conduct said lessons at Longbourn. *Surely, lessons from a master will benefit her immensely,* Darcy considered. *Indeed—a gift to us all.*

~ ~ ~

Darcy found Elizabeth in the formal dining-room speaking with Mrs. Reynolds and several members of the household staff, presumably about that night's dinner. Each and every one of them concentrated upon the tasks before them, hardly aware of his presence. He cleared his throat to command everyone's immediate attention, and signalled that they should all leave the room.

Elizabeth looked at him momentarily before resuming her activities. He approached her, placed his hands about her waist, leaned forward, and kissed her along her slender neckline.

"Mr. Darcy, what are you doing? Why did you dismiss the servants? There is so much left undone and little time remaining."

He made a cursory glance about the room. "Everything looks splendid. I believe you have outdone yourself, Mrs. Darcy. I beseech you to allow Mrs. Reynolds to take over from here."

"I will not ask that of Mrs. Reynolds. What do you need?" Elizabeth asked impatiently, as she attempted to remove his hands from her waist to resume her task.

"I need a private audience with you…, upstairs."

"I think not..., as you can see, I have dressed for dinner already—I believe it is time you do the same."

"Precisely, this is why I need you," his voice trailed off with the resumption of his amorous ministrations.

"I must attend to this personally. I have some concerns over the seating arrangements."

"Allow me to guess. You wish to make sure that Richard is as far away from Jane as conceivable. Do tell me that Richard will at least be able to dine in the same room as the rest of us."

"That is very amusing, Mr. Darcy. I daresay it is hardly conducive to encouraging me to abandon my task and join you upstairs."

"Then, will you join me in my study. I have a very special gift I wish to give you. I promise not to take up too much of your time." Elizabeth acquiesced. Darcy kissed her before taking her hand and leading her into his study. They arrived to find the room cast in a romantic overtone, dimly lit with only the glow of the burning logs in the fireplace.

Locking the door behind them, he led her to his desk, lifted her to its surface, and began kissing her passionately.

Endeavouring to keep up her resoluteness, Elizabeth whispered, "Though this is nice, I really have little time to spare, especially if this is all you had in mind."

"Are you suggesting that you do not feel the same passion for me that I feel for you?" He spoke the words in a low, sultry tone that nearly took her breath away.

She hesitated. She gulped. "No...."

"Then, why protest?" Darcy asked between light brushes of his lips against hers. Sensing some reluctance, "I will stop if that is your wish. Do you wish that I stop?"

"No—yes..., I find it completely disarming when you are near me like this. You know it too."

"Disarming," he whispered in her ear, the warmth of his

breath slowly melted all her resistance, "that sounds promising."

"Please…," escaped her lips. He thoroughly overwhelmed her sensibilities. Her body arched towards his; completely out of sync with her thoughts. *We have a house full of guests…, There is a plethora of matters to attend to before dinner.*

"Please what?"

"Why did you ask me here?"

"I wanted to give you this." Darcy opened his desk drawer and handed her an exquisitely decorated box. Delighted in receiving such a beautiful package, Elizabeth opened it eagerly with some assistance from Darcy. It was a stunning diamond necklace with matching earrings that sparkled more brilliantly than the blaze of the fire.

"These are exquisite. Is this a family heirloom?"

"No—I had these commissioned especially for you, my love."

Elizabeth kissed him softly on his cheek in gratitude. "Thank you, William. I shall cherish these always."

Darcy took the gift box from her hand, set it aside, and resumed his sensuous kisses. "Please say that you will join me upstairs. I need you, now."

"I am sorry to disappoint you, but I am afraid I must get back to things." Seeing his considerable frustration she placed her hand along side of his chin. "Do not look so forlorn, my love. We have all night, and I have yet to present my gift to you."

It was the evening before Christmas. Everyone at Pemberley, family and servants alike, were in a joyous mood. As Darcy had mentioned, his wife had indeed outdone herself. The dinner party was a glorious affair. Lady Ellen was able to breathe a deep sigh of relief with the addition of her family at Pemberley. The contrast between the Fitzwilliam family and the Bennet family was so stark, and never more so than when they all assembled in the grand dining-room. It was not as though there was anything wrong with that. Both families behaved as spoke of their social classes. The Fitzwilliam family being of the upper order, the highest level of society, displayed exemplary behaviour in style and in custom. The Bennet family, though partly of the second class as a result of the former and the current masters of Longbourn, were further drawn down on the social ladder with their roots so deeply entrenched in trade. The reality was that neither good taste, elegance of style, nor manner could alter Society's rigid class system—a fact that was deeply ingrained in Lady Ellen's psyche.

For that evening, despite a host of servants to attend to their every need, the Fitzwilliam family was forced to be less formal, while the Bennet family was obliged to be even more so; all in all, resulting in a fairly pleasant evening for everyone concerned.

~ ~ ~

The day after Christmas, Lord and Lady Matlock, Lord Robert, and his wife returned to their home before heading off to town for the seating of Parliament in January, and their annual Twelfth Night Masquerade Ball. The Gardiners returned to town, with promises from their nieces to spend some time with them in a few weeks.

Lord Harry and Georgiana returned to Staffordshire with the knowledge that their separation from the Darcys would be very short-lived, for they all planned to return to town in time for the ball.

The Hertfordshire guests were obliged to return home, as well. Every one of them was pleased with having had the opportunity to visit the Darcys at Pemberley. With the notable exception of a couple, no one had any cause to repine. The exceptions, Mrs. Bennet and Mr. Collins, were quite perplexed, for despite all their many not so subtle hints, invitations to attend the Matlock's ball had not been extended, nor had there been any mention of them being invited to town during the Season.

Jane and Richard were all that remained of the guests. As anxious as Elizabeth was to see Richard gone as well, she felt it a hopeless cause. Did she dare insist that one leave and not the other?

The Fitzwilliam family's presence had provided a somewhat welcome cessation of Richard's attentions to Jane, albeit short-lived as they were there only a few days. Elizabeth had to admit that her sister's spirits had improved immensely over the past weeks. Even with the separation from her husband and the girls, Jane seemed nowhere near as forlorn as Elizabeth believed that she might have been in a similar situation.

Elizabeth began to question the wisdom of inviting her sister to spend the Season in town with her. She did so with the belief that Jane and her entire family would join them. And perhaps it was to be so. She had to hold out hope. The prospect of her dear sister succumbing to Colonel Richard Fitzwilliam's charms was too much for her to contemplate.

~ ~ ~

Jane was certainly mindful of her relationship with her husband. She believed him to be a respectable man whose interests did not always coincide with hers. It seemed to her that his sole interest was in her being a mother to his children. Though it was a task that she also enjoyed very much, she wanted a little more. She wanted a Season in town, a portion of her youth that she had forgone while working as a governess in Scotland.

To Elizabeth's increasing vexation, Richard and Jane had formed a society of mutual admiration. They were far too often in one another's sole company. She hated seeing her sister being drawn in by such a man. Jane did nothing to discourage his attentions. She seemed blinded by fascination. There was no doubt that Jane was pleased with the distraction he provided. The two seemed to Elizabeth, as always contriving excuses to be constantly in each other's presence. Jane even endeavoured to capture Richard's likeness on canvas. The unveiling, yet, another opportunity for him to fawn over her, and flatter her ego with praises.

The moment of the unveiling was fraught with eager anticipation. Whatever the outcome, everyone felt obliged to offer high praise. The entire time she worked on her masterpiece, no one was allowed to look, save Jane and her maid, who served as her assistant.

Richard was amazed by his portrayal, as was Darcy and Elizabeth. He moved to Jane's side to admire his likeness up close. A full minute had passed before he spoke.

"You have undersold your talents, Mrs. Eliot. The likeness is incredible." He raised Jane's hand to his lips and imparted a lingering kiss. "The painting is worthy of the Halls of Pemberley, if I must say so myself. What say you, Darcy?"

"Indeed, it is incredible," Darcy praised. "It is a credit to your talents that you have captured his likeness in so flattering a fashion."

"Mr. Darcy, I fear you are simply teasing me," Jane meekly exclaimed.

"Oh, no! No, it is very good," Darcy replied.

"I agree most wholeheartedly, Jane," Elizabeth added in sincerity, "when did you become so talented?"

"For the past couple of years, I admit to having little else to do in my fleeting moments of free time."

"Let me assure you," Darcy said, "you have employed your time and attention to your art most advantageously."

"Here, here!" Richard added. "Let us all have a drink to toast the very beautiful Mrs. Eliot and her many wonderful talents."

It did not end there. Jane and Richard could always be seen walking the paths of Pemberley for hours during the day, even amidst the coldness of December. This too struck Elizabeth as particularly strange, for she never knew her sister to be such a great walker.

The easiness of which the two were known to associate was too disconcerting for Elizabeth to bear. That combined with the way Jane's husband left Pemberley continued to bother Elizabeth. If; indeed, there was trouble in the marriage, as Elizabeth had begun to suspect, the last thing her sister needed was Richard's shoulder to cry upon.

How could she confront Jane with her apprehensions or even Richard, for that matter? Elizabeth decided it was better to speak directly with Darcy about her worries, and perhaps persuade him to invite his cousin to leave Pemberley, before things grew out of hand. Alas, it seemed her every concern fell upon deaf ears.

~ ~ ~

Darcy and Elizabeth loved their early morning horseback rides along the many natural trails of Pemberley Woods. Amidst the tranquil setting, the calm serenity, they often had a sense that they were the only two people in the world. Such peacefulness could not be enjoyed that morning, however. They were not alone. Richard and Darcy also enjoyed a habit of riding out each morning when they were together at Pemberley and Matlock. Then too, there was Jane.

The four of them rode along at a leisurely pace that allowed them to converse amongst themselves with ease. Mindful of his wife's objection to seeing Richard and her sister spend as much time in each other's company as they did, Darcy endeavoured to distract his cousin with a suggestion to race ahead, thus providing Jane and Elizabeth with a chance to talk. The condemning looks, the unspoken animosity, and feigned politeness that Elizabeth demonstrated towards her husband's cousin and best friend had become increasingly evident to Jane, as well.

"Lizzy, might I ask why you dislike Colonel Fitzwilliam as you do?"

"Jane, I do not dislike him as much as I do not trust him. I have noticed that he spends considerable time with you. What is he about?"

"Was it not just a few weeks past that you thought the same on the amount of time he spent with Mr. Darcy?"

"As well I did." Elizabeth replied rather hastily in her own defence, "Nevertheless, you have failed to answer my question."

"You may choose to ask me any question you like, dear sister. That does not obligate me to answer."

"Jane, you must see that I ask simply out of concern for your welfare."

"Of course—but you need not make yourself uneasy on my behalf. I assure you, I know what I am about. Colonel Fitzwilliam is a very decent and amiable man, perhaps even worthy of *your* trust. Is he not your own husband's closest friend?"

At the same time, Darcy and Richard shared a similar dialogue.

"Are you suggesting that I spend less time with Mrs. Eliot out of concern for her own welfare, or is this simply to appease your wife?"

"Does it really matter? You can have no serious intentions towards Mrs. Eliot."

"Serious intentions? I seriously intend her no harm. She is a handsome woman with a certain angelic charm about her. When have you ever known me not to find that to be an appealing combination?"

"Even if she were single, I would caution you not to trifle with her. The fact that she is married makes the idea of you trifling with her affections even more abhorrent."

"My intentions towards the lady are honourable!"

"See that they remain that way," Darcy commanded, as he moved to race forward on his horse, outpacing Richard by some distance.

An hour or so later, the foursome gathered in the breakfast-room. The exceptionally bright morning sunshine did nothing to lift the heavy gloominess that filled the air. No one was speaking to anyone. Elizabeth remained behind once she saw that Richard was in no particular hurry to get on with his day. She tried unsuccessfully to persuade Jane to join her in her sitting-room for a morning of mending and a bit of browsing the latest fashion magazines in preparation for the upcoming trip to town. With no luck, Elizabeth abandoned her watch over her sister and joined Darcy in his study. She thought once again to try to persuade him to encourage Richard to leave.

"I will not ask Richard to leave Pemberley. He is as close to me as a brother. Short of a horrendous transgression, he is always welcome in my home. I would no more ask him to leave than I would ever expect you to ask that Jane leaves."

"Jane! You dare to compare my most beloved sister to your cousin!"

"Is the reason that you are so anxious to see Richard take his leave, not on account of your concern for your sister?"

"Richard is simply taking advantage of my sister's good nature and her susceptibility. She has not had to fend off men with his particular brand of charms. He is a notorious flirt—dare I even call him a rake!"

Darcy was taken aback by her accusation. "Perhaps you have read too many romance novels. On what basis do you level such a complaint against him? And what do you know of what your sister has had to fend off?"

"I have spoken to Jane. I suspect she is blinded by his amiability. I am simply not convinced that your cousin's motives are innocuous."

"Elizabeth, they are consenting adults. You must allow them the ability to know their own minds."

"My sister is vulnerable, and HE is not to be trusted!"

"Why are you so biased against Richard?"

"You can hardly be of any doubt. I had no idea that in marrying you, I was also committing myself to a future with him."

"Elizabeth, you have always known how close Richard and I are." Darcy went on to remind her that Richard was willing to stand up for them when no one in his family would. "He has always been there for me."

"Now you have me."

"Yes, and you have your sister Jane. I would never venture to interfere in that relationship."

"So, is that how you view my concerns…, as interfering in your relationship with your cousin?"

The power that Elizabeth held over her husband was immense. He had long since conceded that fact to himself. However, her insistence that he asks Richard from his home was not at all reasonable in his estimation and thus, not to be taken seriously. Accepting Richard at his word, Darcy believed all her suspicions against his cousin were unfounded. To act as she suggested would be tantamount to alienating the one person that had been with him, through good and through bad, all his life. The possibility that in not heeding his wife's demands, he was risking her alienation was simply not a consideration.

Darcy crossed the room to close the distance between

them. He gently cradled her chin and raised her face to meet his gaze.

"Where are you going with this conversation? You are most important to me. You must never doubt that, my love. That does not diminish Richard's importance. You know that Georgiana, Richard, and you are the three people whom I hold most dear in this world. Would you really ask that I relinquish the lifelong bond that he and I share?

"Richard will not remain with us much longer; I can assure you of that. Soon, he will tire of my fully domesticated ways and seek more lively companionship."

"I can hardly wait for that day," she reluctantly conceded. "When exactly do you suppose that will be?"

He kissed the top of his wife's head gently before resting his chin thereupon. As he ran his hands along her shoulders and caressed her arms, he said, "Let us take things one day at a time. We travel to town in but a few days. We will get through your first Season as Mrs. Darcy and all that entails. When we return to Pemberley for the summer, Richard will have grown completely weary of us. It will be just us two for a while, perhaps till our first child is born. Will that not be wonderful?"

Darcy had unwittingly touched upon a very sensitive subject for Elizabeth. Though it had not been six months, her disappointment in not becoming with child yet weighed in the back of her mind, more than she dared to admit to anyone, even to her husband.

~ *Chapter 4* ~
What the Heart Wants

E ven though nearly a week off, she suffered some trepidation over her first appearance amidst society as Mrs. Elizabeth Darcy. The two of them appeared together out and about London society too many times to keep track of over the past two years. Appearing together as a newly-wed couple cast an entirely different light on the matter. Before, HE engendered the hopes and dreams of many of the over-eager mamas and their unmarried daughters. SHE accompanied his younger sister as a paid companion. Many of those with whom the Darcys associated at that time had barely acknowledged her at all. Lord and Lady Matlock's society, the only society that Darcy felt most obliged to turn up at, composed entirely of the highest echelons —the ruling class and the wealthiest of gentlemen.

Even Darcy's close friend, Charles Bingley, his family having earned their fortune in trade, did not gain acceptance in Lord and Lady Matlock's circle, despite his marriage to Lady Grace. The prospect of limited contact with one of her least favourite people, Bingley's sister Caroline, promised the one blessing to Elizabeth. However, as the Darcys were not bound by the same societal dictates as Lord and Lady Matlock, some contact with the Bingleys, specifically Caroline Bingley, seemed inevitable.

Both Darcys looked forward to finding themselves in the company of Charles and his lovely wife with enthusiasm. Elizabeth and Lady Grace had kept up a steady correspondence with one another over the past year. Elizabeth ceded her aversion to Caroline's society as a small price to pay for the sake of her friendship with Lady Grace. Elizabeth suffered mixed emotions as to how Jane might get along with the Bingleys. If she relied solely upon her sister's expressed sentiments, she had no cause for concern. Nevertheless, feeling as she did, more than ever, that Jane rarely shared her true sentiments with anyone, Elizabeth trusted her own instincts to know better. Little more could occur, but to cross that bridge when they came upon it.

During their time together at Pemberley, Elizabeth and Lady Ellen did much to prepare her wardrobe for the Season. All of her things arrived in town at Darcy House in advance of her coming. The addition of Jane to the party was a cause for many last-minute activities that had not been anticipated, posing somewhat of a conundrum. Jane had no inclination to spend Mr. Eliot's money as freely as required. She felt just as reluctant in accepting such generosity from her sister.

Even in such ostensibly trifling matters as that, Jane sensed a growing divide between her world and that of her sister. In that situation, it simply did not matter. The expense must be borne—even if by Mrs. Darcy. Lady Ellen had accepted Jane into her circle. Though she, being a gentleman's daughter and married to a gentleman hardly recommended her. Neither of the gentleman's families had any significant fortune to speak of. Lady Ellen deemed Jane as tolerable enough, and capable of presenting herself well amongst the elite. Besides, as the sister of Mrs. Elizabeth Darcy, she must surely look the part.

As regarded the other matter of contention between the two sisters, they agreed to disagree over Jane's friendship with Colonel Fitzwilliam. To Elizabeth's relief, when they all arrived in London from Pemberley, they parted company with Richard. He went ahead to Matlock House. Even better, from Elizabeth's perspective, they spent very little time in his company during the first week in town. Alas, they received less pleasant news that Mr. Eliot would not join them in town in time for the Matlock's Twelfth Night Ball. An elderly acquaintance of his was ailing. Mr. Eliot preferred to remain in Hertfordshire, readily available during his friend's time of need.

~ ~ ~

The opulence and splendour of Matlock House seemed as magnificent as Elizabeth remembered it exactly one year ago, that night. That occasion held such magical memories for her, for it was then that she first experienced Darcy's intimate touch, and his lips pressed softly against her skin.

The vast and colourful array of costumes and masks provided quite a degree of anonymity for the guests. Intimately ensconced amongst the jubilant congregation, Darcy spoke to his wife in a manner that only she would hear.

"I feel it is incumbent upon me to tell you that it is my intention to remain close to you this evening." He raised her hand to his lips and bestowed a soft kiss. "I fully intend to make love to you several times throughout the night."

"Are you reading my mind, Mr. Darcy?"

"I believe so; which leads me to a second pronouncement. I insist that you dance with no one but me," he then kissed the palm of her hand, "for I am not of a mind to wait about when the mood arises."

"You will likely suffer disappointment in that, I fear. Jane is our guest. She scarcely knows anyone here. I find it unpardonable to consider abandoning her."

"She knows Richard." Elizabeth looked at her husband with dismay. Before she managed a response, none other than Richard himself had approached Jane to request the next set. Upon her acceptance, he graciously extended his arm to her and proceeded to lead her away from Darcy and Elizabeth, to speak with her alone, whilst they awaited their dance.

Darcy could see that his wife was not pleased with the development. Despite her truce with Jane, it was evident that she was not in favour of her continuing friendship with Richard. Elizabeth proceeded to set off after her sister, when Darcy grabbed hold of her hand and would not release it. "What exactly do you intend to do, my love?"

"I mean to put a stop to this foolishness—once and for all."

"Your sister is not a child," he scolded. "I fear you risk alienating her if you continue to distrust her to know her own mind."

"I do feel a certain responsibility towards protecting her, as should you."

"She is in no harm from Richard. You, on the other hand, are in great danger from me." Darcy kissed Elizabeth along her slender neckline.

"Sir, remember yourself please. What do you suppose people might say?"

"That I cannot keep my hands off of my wife…, is that so bad?"

"Our first public appearance in town—I should say so!"

"Ah—but our identities are fully disguised. To unknowing eyes, we might be anyone." Darcy kissed her hand. "Come with me, my love."

Elizabeth's passions stirred from the moment he closed the door. She watched as he turned the key in the lock; then as he approached her, each step bringing them closer and closer, till there was little space between them. Her innermost thoughts sang out; *this will be a night I shall never forget.*

Masks aside, Elizabeth thought of him as being the most devastatingly handsome man she had ever seen. She could not break her eyes away from his beautifully alluring smile. He took her hand in his and raised it to his lips, exciting feelings deep inside of her. *This is no ordinary kiss. How is it that he has never kissed me like this before?*

He whispered in her ear his mission; to love her as he had never done. With no one other than the two of them locked inside the room, there was hardly a need to whisper. He meant to captivate her. He did. The sultry sensation of his breath on her skin was riveting.

Darcy recalled the first time that Elizabeth and he were alone in that very room. Then, she was his forbidden fruit. Forever more, his wife—the love of his life. Darcy stood in the same spot as before, so close to her with his hands around her waist, holding her tightly.

The light cast by the fire rendered just enough brightness to glimpse her face, as he teased her with soft kisses. He kissed her gently upon her forehead…, her cheeks. He lightly brushed his lips against hers, tenderly and reverently, as if it were their first kiss.

She looked amazing—as beautiful as he ever recalled; draped in diamonds that sparkled even in the faint light. He spoke her name softly, "Elizabeth." The cessation of his incredibly sweet lips upon her skin left her wanting more. She slowly opened her eyes to his penetrating gaze.

He swept his fingers against her neck and along her jaw. He slowly traced the side of her face to her cheek and ran his thumb over her lower lip, resting there. "Do you ever fantasise, my love?"

A quiet gulp—a missed heartbeat; she was rendered speechless by the sensual melody of his voice. *Do I ever!* She found her voice. "Fantasise? Of what?"

"Do you fantasise of the two of us making passionate love on this night?" He kissed her along the neckline. "In this house," he kissed her along the other side. "In this room," he lifted her onto the edge of the desk and began a passionate assault along her soft shoulders and enticing décolletage.

He whispered, "I must confess that it is all I could think of all day... I wanted you so badly when we were last here." He lowered her gown as much as he needed to reveal her bosom. He began caressing her gently, as he imparted a deep, passionate kiss. "If you had any idea how badly I wanted you even then." His voice trailed off again as he recaptured her lips. He began raising the hem of her gown to her waist. "I want you so much more now, my love."

He massaged her, gently stroked her, and steady to his purpose, pleased her. "Yes!" Endless soft cries of *yes* reverberated throughout the room.

At length, one accommodated the other, affecting a steady and sensuous union.

Every sound, the orchestra, the party goers just outside the door, even the crackle of the fire faded. She could distinguish nothing other than the sound of her name repeatedly from his lips. Their bodies in exquisite harmony, both gave into the feelings of their deep desire for each other as he loved her more passionately than she had yet to experience.

Time enough passed. He arranged his own attire and assisted her likewise. "You are exquisite, Elizabeth." He bestowed a lingering last kiss to her lips before replacing her mask. "You mean everything to me."

Back inside the grand ballroom, Lord Harry and Georgiana stood with Richard and Jane upon the Darcys' return. Georgiana had searched the room in vain during most of their absence. She began to fret that her sister might have fallen ill and left the ball early. Coming across Richard and Jane when she did, provided her with some level of comfort.

"Elizabeth, I have looked for you for over an hour. Where have the two of you been all this time?"

"Georgiana, I gave my wife a tour of Matlock House."

"A tour? Why on earth would Elizabeth need a tour of the house, when she stayed here with me for nearly three weeks?" Georgiana asked.

"My dear Lady Georgiana, I believe I am up for a tour of Matlock House as well…, if you will do me the honour," Lord Harry suggested. Allowing no time for a response, he eagerly began leading her away.

The Darcys' second tour of Matlock House barely ended in time for supper. Though quite famished, they ate quickly and sparsely. The two aimed to resume their mission. Darcy had promised Elizabeth yet another tour of a different part of the house—the family wing.

~ ~ ~

The growing familiarity between Richard and Jane did not go unnoticed by Lady Matlock. But more than that, she noticed how much it bothered her niece Elizabeth. Upon observing Elizabeth's preoccupation with the two of them, whenever they were together, she ventured to speak with her about it.

Her Ladyship's advice to Elizabeth was simply put—do not be concerned. She was sure that there was nothing untoward in the relationship. She reminded Elizabeth once more that her son was a very determined flirt, but he would never harm

Jane, who was like family to them all. Elizabeth thought of Lady Ellen as far too partial when it came to her younger son, especially in thinking that he did not have nefarious intentions towards Jane. She could not help but wonder why she was the only one who seemed concerned for her sister's welfare.

Lady Ellen had far greater concerns. She was increasingly perplexed as to how to sponsor Elizabeth amongst the *ton*, if a bushel of tradesmen were a part of the package.

In reality, it was Elizabeth's third Season in town. The first two were as Georgiana's paid companion. This one was truly her own. Everyone would be eager to know more of the woman who had captured the long sought Fitzwilliam Darcy of Pemberley. The first impression should not be that he had married his former employee, but rather that he had married the beautiful and charming Miss Elizabeth Bennet of Hertfordshire. Lady Ellen determined that Elizabeth would be favourably received by all.

For the third time in as many days, a group of society women sat around in Lady Ellen's parlour having tea and biscuits while engaged in an awkward discussion, where Lady Ellen put the distinction between Elizabeth herself and her mother's side of the family forth. The audience varied, but the conversation remained much the same.

"You have seen the dear young woman on numerous occasions already. You have dined with her in this very home. You are able to judge for yourselves how she will comport herself within our circle."

Lady Bigelow was the eldest and most fastidious of all those assembled. Whenever she spoke, the others tended to listen. "During said times," she began, "the distinction of rank was clearly preserved. She did not present herself as one who aspired beyond her station as a paid companion. Now, she has had a glimpse of wealth and privilege. Her manners are likely altered indeed."

"She suffers no such pretentiousness," Lady Ellen offered. "She is entirely virtuous and courageous; both she and her lovely sister did what they must in securing reputable positions to support their family, after the most horrid fate of them being cast aside with the death of their father, a country gentleman."

"A *poor* country gentleman," Lady Gwendolyn gently reminded everyone.

Lady Elise had spent enough time in Elizabeth's company to consider her a friend, with the advent of her marriage to Darcy. Typically, she had little to say, but in that situation, she sought to lend her support. "A gentleman still," she stated, startling everyone in so doing. She continued, "Her family was thrown from their home due to the unfortunate circumstances of an entail."

"Really Ellen—you cannot be serious in promoting this unequal alliance!" Lady Gwendolyn spoke out, disregarding Lady Elise's remarks with a dismissive wave of her hand.

"Birth and pedigree might be overriding factors to wealth. I suppose," remarked Lady Sumner, as she peered over her spectacles.

"Is she educated? Who was her governess?" Lady Bigelow demanded.

"The family had no governess," responded Lady Ellen.

"Five daughters brought up at home with no governess! Why, I have never heard of such a thing. Their mother must have been quite a slave to their education!" Lady Bigelow exclaimed.

"I suppose she had the benefit of the masters," added Lady Sumner in a more reasoned voice, eager as she was to find any redeeming factor in Elizabeth's perceived educational shortcoming.

Placing her fine porcelain cup aside with a faint clatter that spoke of her increasing annoyance, Lady Ellen stated, "No, not one. Though, I suppose they might have, had they so desired."

"Yet another crack in the armour of elite society, I say," voiced another of the guests.

Lady Augusta, a particular friend of Lady Ellen's and a firm believer of equality of fortune and station as paramount in any alliance, stated her opinion. "Yes, Darcy chose a wife who is a great beauty. However, he might have chosen someone as equally beautiful and every bit as courageous and virtuous amongst our circle. I say it is just another example of him thumbing his nose at society, as he has always done, and I daresay might continue to do even now that he has married so recklessly."

"Precisely! Leave it to your nephew to turn his nose up to society's expectations in this manner. To put us all out with his general disdain," Lady Gwendolyn complained.

The possibility that Lady Ellen might endure, for even a second longer, any criticism of her beloved nephew, akin to her as her own son, was unfathomable. She sought to end that line of discussion post-haste. "You should not feel that way. Gentlemen will be gentlemen, as most of you are all too aware. Nevertheless, if you persist in stating your opinion of my nephew in such an unguarded fashion, it is better that we reconsider any further association."

As Lord Matlock was a very prominent and influential member of the House of Lords, Lady Ellen did not doubt her sway amongst the *ton* in the least bit.

Another woman imparted, "Alas, the heart wants what the heart wants, and I suppose that his wife is his heart's desire. At least he chose a gentlewoman." *Albeit she was his former employee*, she thought but did not dare to voice aloud.

"What is done is done," Lady Sumner rejoined.

"Indeed, it is done. You and I have long enjoyed one another's society. It is my greatest wish that we shall always continue to do so. I will rely upon your word that young Mrs. Darcy is worthy and quite capable of conducting herself as expected amongst our circle," Lady Bigelow declared.

"Indeed, we must welcome her. One can hardly blame the young woman. Why should she not have sought such an advantageous situation in life?" Lady Gwendolyn remarked dryly.

As one lady acquiesced, so did all of them till everyone gathered was in accord. The group of ladies having departed from her home, Lady Ellen wearily lamented to her daughter-in-law Elise, on the many trials she faced in fostering Elizabeth's acceptance amongst their circle. One only needed to remind the other that it was a battle on both fronts as they recalled her efforts to persuade Elizabeth to appear in Royal Court. As the Bennets were not high enough on the social ladder to presume to royal recognition, it was a matter that had never entered Elizabeth's mind. She was not inclined to agree, especially since the invitation had not been extended to Jane. A hard-fought battle of wills ensued. Lady Ellen's staunch insistence upon the importance of such an honour for her, as the wife of Fitzwilliam Darcy and one day the mother of Pemberley's heir, persuaded Elizabeth to go along with her Ladyship's wishes.

~ *Chapter 5* ~
A Striking Resemblance

The countdown to the night of the highly prestigious gala at Matlock House had begun. The guest list included some of the most distinguished families amongst London's elite society; the same women Lady Ellen had successfully persuaded to promote the alliance. Her Ladyship visited with Elizabeth at Darcy House. She wanted to share her intimate thoughts on a number of the prominent people whom Elizabeth would be meeting.

Elizabeth had grown increasingly perturbed leading up to that day, over what she perceived as an egregious slight to her own acquaintances. She could no longer refrain from speaking her mind.

"I beg your pardon, Lady Ellen. You have said nothing of having extended an invitation to my uncle and aunt Gardiner. As they live here in town, I certainly expect that they too will be in attendance."

"Elizabeth, my dear, you know me well enough to understand why that will never be." She placed her hand upon Elizabeth's hand. "I associate with your aunt and uncle when I am in your home. I find them quite charming, in fact, but that does not in any way suggest that I am likely ever to entertain them in my home."

"I fear that I do not understand. How can you expect me to ignore this slight? I daresay my aunt and uncle are every bit as respectable as any of your haughty acquaintances. Why, I contend that you not accepting the Gardiners is tantamount to you not accepting me."

"Elizabeth, do not be ridiculous. Of course, I accept you as Fitzwilliam's wife. Have I not spent the past three months, almost exclusively, to that very cause?"

"If the cause that you speak of, is the time you have spent polishing me up to fit your world, then you are correct. However, my sharing your world does not make me inclined to ignore my own family in any way. You know how important the Gardiners are to me."

"My world, as you put it, is your husband's world too. Though my nephew and you seem comfortable straddling the lines of social class and associating with tradesmen, I do not share your views, not now nor will I ever. Coming to terms with that is in your best interest, my dear."

The two women were at a stand-off. Though Jane was present during the entirety of the discussion, she could only observe their interaction in wonderment. Elizabeth declared that she did not wish to engage the society of those who chose to look down upon her relatives, simply because they were in trade. Lady Ellen beseeched her to be reasonable. Failing that, she pleaded her case to her nephew.

Darcy had lived his entire life with the same notions as his aunt in this matter; it did not take much for her to convince him to speak with Elizabeth—the class distinctions must be upheld, even if his wife did not agree. Yes—he made exceptions, and yes—he admired some of her relatives, but Elizabeth could not expect his relatives to cast aside beliefs that were their guiding principles and deeply rooted amongst the *ton*.

For the first time in his married life, Darcy felt obliged to choose the side of his aunt over his wife's. It was a position he loathed being forced into. It was a conversation he never wished to have.

Elizabeth was in the drawing-room arranging a large bouquet in an exquisitely detailed oriental vase, when Darcy found her. He reckoned there was no reason to beat around the bush. He came straight to the point in arguing his aunt's case.

"You are asking me to change who I am—to turn my back on my own relatives, and for what? To appease those who are so wholly unconnected to me."

"No—that is not what I am asking of you. I am asking that you be more tolerant of the opinions of others, even those beliefs that contradict your own. My aunt is only trying to help you to navigate in this world that you have entered pursuant to our marriage.

"There are expectations of you as my wife that are different from those had you married someone of lesser fortune and privilege. To do that which is outside of your comfort level is not to violate your principles, Elizabeth."

Recalling himself to an eerily similar conversation that he had shared with his aunt and uncle, he considered the irony that he had expressed those exact words—of course the difference being the ensuing real connection. "As regards your connections, you are now wholly connected with Lord and Lady Matlock. You should endeavour to find a way to embrace that."

A heated discussion between Darcy and Elizabeth on tolerance ensued.

"It is so like YOU," she accused, "to take your aunt's side in this matter. I am forced to recall how you barely tolerated me upon our initial acquaintance."

"Elizabeth, you are being unfair. I have always admired you. You know that too." Darcy persisted. "I will not allow you to make this about me. It is your seeming intolerance of my family's principles that I wish to discuss. Must I remind you that the notion of tolerance, as you so adamantly espouse works both ways? I only ask that you not be intolerant of my aunt simply because she is intolerant of yours.

"Furthermore, if you insist upon making this about my former sentiments," Darcy questioned, "am I expected to cast all my beliefs aside and embrace all yours fully, whereas you expect to cast none of yours aside?" Elizabeth remained silent throughout the rest of his speech, but the ill-humoured look on her face and the steadiness in her shoulders led him to soften his approach.

Darcy lovingly ran his fingers through his wife's loose curls and kissed her upon her forehead. "Elizabeth, I beg of you. Please compromise with Lady Ellen on this. Meet her halfway. She will never do anything to offend you personally, I assure you of that. In this instance, she is only looking out for your— for our interests amongst the *ton*."

Elizabeth could hardly wait to escape her husband's presence that afternoon. *How dare he ask me to compromise my principles for anyone?* She needed to see her aunt. She did not even bother to invite Jane to accompany her to Gracechurch Street.

As expected, she found a very kind and sympathetic audience. Mrs. Gardiner listened with patience as Elizabeth paced back and forth about the room voicing her complaints on the overbearing and haughty Lady Matlock, her pretentious and arrogant family, and most of all, her dreadfully insensitive nephew.

Mrs. Gardiner was not at all surprised by Elizabeth's visit and the ensuing tirade over Lady Matlock. In fact, she wondered what had taken her niece so long. Mrs. Gardiner had observed Lady Matlock's increasing abhorrence of the Bennet family in December. She also noted that Lady Matlock did all that she could in masking her disdain. Mrs. Gardiner and Lady Matlock spent time together with no animosity at all between them. Still, she was completely mindful of the fact that her Ladyship's kindness at Pemberley might very well extend to Darcy House, but certainly no further than that and most especially, not amongst the highest circles of the *ton*.

She offered her niece the following counsel.

"You must consider the doors that this alliance with Mr. Darcy, and by extension his family, have opened to you. Even if all that means nothing to you, think of what it might mean to your unborn children, the future generation of Pemberley?"

Elizabeth had calmed considerably since her arrival. She now sat beside her aunt. Mrs. Gardiner rested her hand upon her niece's hand. "The attitudes of society will change in their own pace. In fact, they are already beginning to change. Is not your marriage to Mr. Darcy evidence of that?

"You must admit that your Fitzwilliam relations are very amiable to your uncle and me when we are guests at Pemberley. I do not hold them in any less regard because they choose to observe the distinctions of rank and privilege in their own home. That is the way of their world. I recommend that you do not judge them too harshly either, my dear. And never take offence against them on our behalf."

Mrs. Gardiner's words left Elizabeth with much to consider. By the time that Elizabeth prepared to return to Darcy House, she had been not quite as angry as before with her husband for not taking a stand in support of her sentiments, against those of his aunt. Darcy was nowhere to be found upon Elizabeth's return. She wanted to continue their discussion. She learned from his valet that he had ventured out.

As it happened, he left their home shortly after her hasty departure, for a round of drinks at White's with Richard. Darcy felt somewhat conflicted by his admonishments to his wife. He had never truly been a fan of society—he was only interested in spending the Season in town for her sake. He confided in his cousin that he had second thoughts in having spoken to Elizabeth, as he had.

"I should not worry so much, if I were you, Cousin. For what it is worth, I say you did the right thing. I know how little you care for society, but to live amidst its censure is no trifling matter, especially for a man of your station."

"You might have a point, but ultimately if I wish to see her happy, I must abide by her choice. I have to consider what is best for my marriage, even if it means the loss of your parents." Darcy paused a moment to ponder the options before him. "If my wife and my aunt cannot come together on this matter, I see no other choice than to forego the Season and return to Pemberley. After all that Lady Ellen has done to support my marriage, I shall not repay her kindness with effrontery."

"Your detractors might say that you are hiding your lovely wife away in Derbyshire to escape the derision that comes about in such an unequal alliance. Why give credence to such speculation? I am sure your wife and my mother will find a way to present a united front."

Darcy sat back in his chair, pondering his wife's reaction to his earlier stance. He asked himself, *do I even dare to hope?*

Later that evening, the two spoke of their contention. He had quite resolved that she must determine their course; the one caveat being that to remain in town and shun his aunt and uncle was not an option.

"I am accountable to no one—no one but you that is, Elizabeth. Should you decide it is best to turn our backs on society that is open to us, but does not embrace your views of what it should be, perhaps we might return to Pemberley forth-with. There we shall remain for the remainder of our days, only to be bothered by those whom you embrace."

"Are you quite certain, dear husband?" Elizabeth asked sardonically; not entirely certain whether he was sincere or simply melodramatic.

"Quite, it is entirely up to you. You know that I love you above all else. I care more for your feelings than I care for those of anyone else in the entire world. If you no longer care for my aunt's society, then so be it."

"It is not as though I wish to shun your aunt or any of your relatives, for that matter," Elizabeth confessed. "I do not wish to come between your family and you. I have given this some thought, and I am willing to go along with Lady Ellen's wishes in this matter. It is her home, I suppose she can invite, or in this case, not invite anyone she chooses."

Therefore, resolved; the Darcys would stay in town for the rest of the Season.

The next day, Elizabeth visited Lady Ellen at her home. They both agreed to put their differences aside. Elizabeth found herself in a similar situation as she was with Jane. In this matter, they simply agreed to disagree.

~ ~ ~

Finding herself the object of strangers' stares certainly was noth-ing new to Elizabeth. Even as the paid companion to Georgiana, her frequent arrivals in Cheapside always drew a fair amount of attention from passers-by on the streets. As Mrs. Darcy, she drew a greater share of such attentions—her carriage, her attire, and her overall appearance being far grander. Elizabeth had grown quite immune to it all. That particular day, a petite young woman with two small boys happened to catch her eye. The curious stranger practically gawked at Elizabeth as the footman handed her down from the elegant Darcy carriage. One of the restless young lads (an adorable little fellow with bright red hair and light freckles), apparently in the stranger's care, tugged at her worn sleeve, effectively diverting her attention from the beautiful lady in the fine carriage.

Completely caught off guard, Elizabeth momentarily halted her descent. *It is no wonder she stares*, Elizabeth considered. *Clean her up, dress her up, and she might easily look like me. What a striking resemblance!*

Elizabeth began to climb the stairs of the Gardiners' home. Her curiosity would not be contained. She paused once again and looked over her shoulder. It seemed her thoughts, as well as those of the stranger, were in sync. Just up the street, the young woman paused and looked over her shoulder as well, to the sight of two amazing eyes staring back at her.

~ ~ ~

It had been more months than she cared to recall since she last thought of him. In a perversely odd sort of fashion, she had begun to think of him as her benefactor of sorts, her protector, perhaps even her guardian angel. Had it not been for his peculiar arrangement with Madam Adele, there was no telling what her life might have been all those years ago, *might still be...*

Everyone around her then told her just how fortunate she was to have been singled out by him. Having resigned herself to spending what she surmised as the best years of her life in a brothel, she begged to differ. There was nothing at all fortunate about her dire situation. Her life was a nightmare, she strongly felt. As days and nights turned into weeks and months, with no visits from him at all, she began to reconsider; especially as she witnessed the degradations experienced time and again by the other young women around her. Being touched and groped by strange men in the openness of the lounges, their bodies ravished and torn in the privacy of the boudoirs. While the others had little choice but to attend theatre regularly, parade and exhibit themselves, all in the effort to drum up more business to earn their keep, she experienced none of that.

Completely set apart from the other women in the establishment, her life was a strange combination of favour and exemption, dread and apprehension, and uncertainty and fear. The more time that passed and he did not come, the more utterly convinced she grew that the exclusive arrangement would end. It was not as though she ever looked forward to his visits. She found him odd and enigmatic. He rarely spoke. He initiated her into her new life gently; she sensed without truly knowing. Shared accounts with the women around her increased her awareness of certain other facts, as well. He had a kind and considerate touch. He exercised extreme caution to prevent any unintended consequences. He was particularly intimate, and yet he never kissed her lips.

If not for her kind spirit and inclination to show the utmost humility and even deference to the other unfortunate women around her, she knew she would not have survived under such circumstances. Indeed, she feared she would have suffered at their hands. They viewed her as privileged, even if she did not consider herself as such. She knew as well as they did that when the taciturn gentleman changed his mind, she would then be no better off than the rest of them.

The last time she saw him, after months of non-attendance, it was clear that he did not truly wish to be there. As haughty and aloof as she sensed he might be, that was the first time she had observed him so. He was very perfunctory. He was gone within the hour. Speculation of what it all meant rampaged throughout the establishment like wildfire, as those who remained envious of her chided her over the handwriting on the wall.

Months passed with no changes in her situation. Then finally, nearly a full year from when she last saw him, a solicitor arrived wishing to speak with her.

~ ~ ~

With Elizabeth and Georgiana in town for their third Season together, it was as though they had never parted. The notable exception was that they had husbands and were the mistresses of their own homes. They determined to enjoy each other's company as much as possible. The two very often received morning callers together at either Georgiana's home or Darcy House. As Lady Harriette was in residence with her brother and new sister for the Season, Elizabeth and she were in each other's company often.

Lady Harriette was never as considerate of Elizabeth as was her brother. Lord Harry always treated Elizabeth with considerable deference, as she was the best friend of his betrothed. His sister only related to Elizabeth as Georgiana's paid companion; not that she was unpleasant or condescending in any way. Though the two young ladies spent a significant amount of time in each other's company, they rarely engaged in any meaningful dialogue at all.

No one was more surprised than was Lady Harriette by the news of Fitzwilliam Darcy's precipitous marriage to Elizabeth. She had never observed any partiality between the two of them. Perhaps it was more a reflection of her own romanticised notion of Darcy—the exceedingly handsome and highly sought gentleman of the *ton* who might have any woman he chose. It was inconceivable to Lady Harriette that he might have been an admirer of Georgiana's paid companion. The besotted young woman clung to the words of her favourite playwright, *hasty marriage seldom proveth well*. To her way of thinking, it was just a matter of time.

The absence of a shared camaraderie between the two ladies did nothing to dissuade Elizabeth's opinion of Lady Harriette as a great beauty and a highly accomplished young lady. Ever a studier of people, Elizabeth had always noticed the young woman's infatuation with Darcy, even as a source of amusement. Her latest observations convinced her that Lady Harriette had not yet recovered from that ill-fated state. Lady Harriette was a great flirt in general but especially as regarded Darcy. Whether or not by design, he appeared totally oblivious of the young woman.

~ ~ ~

Elizabeth, Jane, and Georgiana planned a shopping excursion. Jane opted out at the last moment, deciding instead to remain at Darcy House that morning. Much to Elizabeth's dismay, Richard arrived just as Georgiana and she got into the carriage. Georgiana's delight proved unmistakable, for she had not seen her cousin for a while. She expressed her joy most readily when he approached the carriage to greet them. Not surprisingly, Elizabeth offered a rather lack-lustre response.

"You do not like Cousin Richard very much, it seems," Georgiana stated, once the carriage began to move away.

"It is not so much that I dislike him, but rather I do not trust his motives towards my sister Jane."

"But surely you trust Jane to know what is in her best interest."

"I am afraid I sense a great alteration in my sister, with our family's change in circumstances. I feel she is somewhat vulnerable."

"Well, you know your sister far better than I; but I am sorry, Elizabeth, I do not share your opinion of my cousin. He is not dishonourable. I know he would do anything in the world for my brother and me. He is extremely loyal, and his loyalty now extends to you."

"I do not know, Georgiana. How I wish he was attached to someone himself; then, Jane might not be such an object of his attentions."

"In wishing to see him attached, you sound very much like Lady Ellen."

"I should hope that I am not as bad as that," Elizabeth remarked. "I cannot help but recall her valiant attempts to find a bride for William, and wonder why she does not apply herself equally to the task of finding a bride for Richard."

"But it is very different for Cousin Richard. He, being the second son of an earl, requires a bride with a substantial fortune to keep him in the lifestyle to which he is accustomed. For Lady Ellen to aspire to make the match would expose her to contempt as being mercenary. Heavens forbid that should happen. No—I am afraid Cousin Richard is on his own as regards finding a wife."

"Perhaps not—perhaps you and I might endeavour to put eligible young women with substantial dowries in his path. How much would you say is the usual price of the second son of an earl?"

"I should say at least 50,000 pounds. I might add that I know quite a few young ladies who meet that criterion, including my dear sister Harriette." Georgiana paused for a moment and contemplated the likelihood of such an alliance. "Though I know she cares not in the slightest for my cousin. I am afraid she has long had her sights on another," she opined in a more sombre tone.

"Then we must look elsewhere," Elizabeth rejoined. She suspected the reason behind Georgiana's mood change and rather wished to redirect the conversation.

The two women made a pact—to find a bride for Richard over the coming months. Whether they were serious or not, Georgiana was glad to escape the subject of Lady Harriette. She had kept her sister's secret, that she believed herself in love with Darcy for nearly a year, even as she attempted to persuade her of the senselessness of it all. Georgiana told Harriette on several occasions that losing her heart to her brother was an exercise in futility, and a complete waste of time for someone with so much to offer. It vexed her that Harriette would not be dissuaded even after Darcy married Elizabeth. It caused somewhat of a rift in the two sisters' affections. Still, a promise was a promise.

Elizabeth and Georgiana returned to Darcy House after a few hours of shopping with absolutely no idea of the delight that awaited them inside. The Bingleys had come to call; all of them, Charles and Lady Grace, Caroline, and even Mr. and Mrs. Hurst. It was the first opportunity for them to see each other since the prior Season.

Elizabeth immediately sensed the unease in the room. All the gentlemen rose upon their entrance. Darcy promptly went to her side.

"Mrs. Darcy, come and welcome our guests."

Bingley approached Elizabeth. "Mrs. Darcy, it is such a pleasure to see you again. Let me be the first amongst us here to offer my congratulations on your marriage to my old friend."

"Why thank you, Mr. Bingley. I am delighted that you have come to call upon us this morning."

"Certainly, and what a pleasure it has been to get reacquainted with your sister, Miss Bennet—sorry Mrs. Eliot. We have been speaking of the good folks of Hertfordshire."

"Indeed." Directing her attention to Lady Grace, who was also standing, Elizabeth approached her with extended arms. "Grace, it is so wonderful to see you again." They embraced.

"I feel the same, Elizabeth. You cannot know how much I have missed both Georgiana and you all these months."

Caroline waxed, "Is this not just lovely, all of us together again..., so like old times."

Caroline attempted to hide her surprise as she noticed the extent of her sister-in-law's friendship with Elizabeth. In truth, Caroline cared very little for Lady Grace. She had been an eager proponent of the alliance with her brother initially, thinking that it might open doors to the Bingleys amongst society's elite. In reality, their standing was as it ever had been before the alliance and perhaps somewhat diminished, at least from Caroline's perspective.

The previous two Seasons in town had provided very limited society with Darcy. Though they had liberal use of Darcy's private box at the theatre, they had yet to share it with him. During the Season of Georgiana's coming out, the Darcys always made use of the Matlock box. During the following Season, after the announcement of Georgiana's engagement, Darcy did not attend the theatre at all.

The prospects for socialising with Darcy seem limited during the upcoming Season as well, for Caroline. On one hand, she would do anything to engage the society of the Matlocks; but even she was beginning to accept that might never be. On the other hand, the prospect of socialising with Elizabeth's Cheapside relatives was unfathomable.

Jane, too, found the familiar exchange between Lady Grace and her sister surprising. She had no idea that they were so intimate, for the subject of Mr. Bingley was never raised between the two of them; other than that he had married so soon after his precipitous departure from Hertfordshire, several years back.

Jane quietly observed the gentle serenity of Lady Grace, the amiability of Mr. Bingley, and the general pretentiousness of his sisters. The scene as it unfolded before her was all too surreal.

Is this a semblance of life that I might have lived? Had he returned to Netherfield Park? Had Lydia not caused a scandal in running away with Mr. Wickham, which resulted in the death of my dear father and our family's home?

If her experience as a governess had taught her anything, it taught her to be sensible. To dwell upon what might have been, what was the point in that? Jane looked at the scene before her and decided it best not to regret anything of the past. Mr. Bingley was a very affable man when in Hertfordshire, and he continued to be so. Any unhappiness he may have suffered in his situation, he did not intend for her to see. She, too, would present herself likewise.

After a short spell, the gentlemen excused themselves from the drawing-room to adjourn to the billiard-room. With Darcy absent from the room, and Elizabeth engaged in conversation with Lady Grace, Caroline seemed to forget herself as she leaped towards condescension in speaking with Georgiana about Elizabeth.

"So what do you think of our dear Eliza, or should I say Mrs. Darcy, Lady Georgiana?" She could barely bring herself to utter her hostess's appellation without a healthy dose of derision.

"I have always loved my sister dearly," said Georgiana. She had hoped to dissuade Caroline from such misguided speech.

"Yes, of course, I imagine she was an extremely loyal companion. But did you really suppose that your companion should one day be your sister?" Caroline continued, apparently missing Georgiana's subtle admonishments.

"Indeed, it is just as it always should have been. My brother loved her longest. A gentleman married to a gentleman's daughter. It is splendid, indeed."

"Surely you jest! She was your own paid companion for Heaven's sake."

"A gentleman's daughter will always be thus, therefore, a suitable match for any gentleman. When has a former position as a lady's companion trumped that?" Suffering not a single bad-tempered bone in her body and certainly never one to judge others based upon their standing in society, despite her own family's steadfast convictions to the contrary, often when it came to Caroline, Georgiana simply could not resist. She continued, "Now, perhaps if my dear brother had married a tradesman's daughter…, that might have given my family quite a pause. Do you not agree, Miss Bingley?"

~ Chapter 6 ~
How Sweet the Taste

In the ensuing weeks, since Lady Ellen's dinner party in honour of the Darcys, the young couple shared a closeness best likened to the early days of their blossoming friendship. They spent hours in the library together, reading and debating, only now, with such pleasurable benefits. When the discussions became too heated, they were always at liberty to defer to their bedroom. They did so with alacrity. Their shared passion was such that Darcy had his staff place a comfortable sofa in the library to replace the two chairs they usually elected to sit in, so that they might be closer to one another. Elizabeth had to admit that she was as enthralled by his touch as he was by hers. She could hardly complain about Darcy's redecoration.

Outside of their home, Darcy was as he ever was in town. It never ceased to amaze her how he could be so loving and completely without reserve when the two of them were alone, and yet so haughty and taciturn with others. She would simply have to learn to accept that he might never comport himself as any other than just that. She had no choice, but to change the way she responded to his behaviour, in such cases.

His change in marital status did little to diminish his attractiveness to the ladies of the *ton*. On the contrary, it seemed to enhance his appeal, or so it appeared to Elizabeth, amongst the sophisticated women of the *ton*. *Had it always been that way, and I simply failed to notice?* She wondered.

As his wife, she could not help but notice as other women tried to catch his eye—perhaps turn his head. Though many of the women realised that they never stood a chance with Darcy before, the fact that he was finally married taught them to reconsider their odds. Obviously, he was not so elusive after all, was their thinking, as well as the talk amongst themselves.

As Georgiana's companion and a maiden, herself, Elizabeth was not privy to the view of society she was beginning to glimpse as Mrs. Darcy. Women who had barely acknowledged her existence before suddenly viewed her with a sense of wonderment. Snide remarks were scarcely concealed. *Lady Middleton's former companion, the wife of Mr. Darcy of Pemberley..., his own employee, living with him all those months..., under his protection..., what else occurred behind the closed doors of Darcy House?*

Though very early in the Season, there were still the occasions of many elegant dinner parties and private balls to attend. Darcy and Elizabeth were enjoying one such evening out. The thinly veiled scrutiny of women in the room was bad enough. However, it was not only the women who observed Mrs. Darcy that evening. She had a strong sense of being watched by someone quite ominous.

At first, it was unsettling. The handsome gentleman standing alone by the doorway had stared at her, since he first came in. She dared not look in his direction; to do so might encourage him. Elizabeth tried to ignore his behaviour, but even as she engaged in conversation with her own party, she felt certain his eyes were upon her.

Sometime during the course of the evening, she had lost sight of him, though the feeling persisted that she was being watched. No wonder she felt as she had. Darcy had left her side for only a short time before she was standing face-to-face with her admirer.

"Mrs. Darcy," the gentleman bowed. "It is a great pleasure to see you again."

Elizabeth was quite taken aback. She had no recollection of ever meeting the gentleman who stood so close to her. Her confusion was noted.

"I see that you do not remember me. I made your acquaintance the Season before last, in this very room. Of course, you were known then as Miss Elizabeth Bennet, the lovely companion to the former Miss Georgiana Darcy."

"Sir, though it may account for why you feel comfortable approaching me in this manner, it does nothing to refresh my memory of the two of us being properly introduced."

"Then I shall rectify that situation at once. I am Sir Walter Tattersail," he said as he bowed once again. "Now that we are properly introduced, might I have the next set?"

Elizabeth consented to his request, and he led her to the dance floor; the entire exchange having been observed by Darcy, as he attempted to make his way to his wife's side, but was waylaid by an old acquaintance.

"Mrs. Darcy, allow me to congratulate you on your new appellation," said Sir Tattersail. "I should not be surprised. It seems Darcy went through great lengths to have you all to himself. However, it is a credit to you—I must say that you were able to find yourself as his wife, as opposed to what he likely had in mind."

"Do you expect me to be flattered, sir? When you have insulted both my integrity, as well as that of my husband," she stated calmly before they were parted by the dance steps.

United once again, he continued, "I beg your pardon, madam, if my words are unflattering. I meant no disrespect to - wards you. However, if you know anything at all about your husband's—shall I say, reputation, then you would know that it is hardly an insult to him. It is an honest observation."

"I must ask that you speak plainly, sir."

"Having shared his home as his sister's companion, you mean to say you know nothing of his reputation?"

Elizabeth gave no answer. Sir Tattersail was convinced he had hit his mark and caused her some disconcert, as she missed a step in the dance. *Good. It serves her right for having re-buffed my attentions the past two Seasons.* He was further in-sulted in believing, as he did, that she pretended never to have even met him.

"Perhaps you are completely ignorant of his, let us say— habits. Let me enlighten you." The dance steps separated them once more, and provided Elizabeth a much-needed opportunity to compose herself, away from his menacing gaze. He resumed his vitriol, as soon as the dance steps brought them together again.

"Your husband kept a less than respectable female com-panion for his sole pleasure for years."

"I am not inclined to believe you, sir," she asserted, as she stopped and faced him directly on the dance floor.

"It is not only true, but widely known amongst those in his closest circle; that and the fact that you bear a most striking re-semblance to the disreputable young woman," he eagerly boas-ted, as he urged her to continue the dance.

Elizabeth refused to let the disagreeable man know just how shaken she was by his words. She continued to move seamlessly through the motions of the dance. *Can this be true? What does this stranger mean by attempting to poison my mind against my husband? How should I feel if indeed it is true that*

he kept a woman? How should I feel knowing she bore a strik-
ing resemblance to me? When exactly did all this occur?

She could not wait to free herself of her objectionable partner. After the dance, she sought the solace of a quiet corner of
the room to mull over the deeply disturbing news. Elizabeth
thought over the past years of her acquaintance with Darcy. She
never had any indication that he might have been involved with
anyone at all. Or had she? Elizabeth suddenly recalled the time
he stayed out all night shortly after her employment began. *Did*
that happen very often? She knew then that it was not her right
to question him. *It was not a matter of concern to me at that*
time, so should it be now? Elizabeth had much to consider.

Though it seemed an eternity in her mind, in fact, it was
mere seconds between the end of the dance with Sir Tattersail
and the arrival of her husband by her side, with refreshment in
hand.

Darcy offered her a glass of wine. "Might I ask what Sir
Tattersail had to say to you that has affected you so?"

"I was only listening to an account of his of a past acquaintance," she responded after taking a sip from her glass.

"I trust that you know not to believe everything you hear."

"I find it interesting that you should say so."

"Elizabeth, I have no secrets that I am unwilling to share
with you. You should bear that in mind."

It seems someone has a guilty conscience. Why should he
suppose that Sir Tattersail was speaking of him? Elizabeth silently asked herself. "This is an interesting discussion for a ballroom, would you not agree?"

"I agree wholeheartedly. However, I will not allow for mis-
understandings between us. You seem upset by your conversation with the gentleman. He is no friend of mine. There is hardly
any telling what might have been said to you."

Sir Tattersail was but one in a long list of gentlemen who had, in one way or another, been aggrieved by Darcy over the years. Not in business, however, but in Darcy's blatant disregard for him. The Fitzwilliam Darcys of the world and their ilk were often the bane of his existence, as they looked down upon him and others of his social strata. That Darcy had married his sister's companion was the ultimate irony. Taking advantage of the opportunity to cause trouble in paradise while killing two birds with one stone, served to smooth his ruffled feathers immensely.

"Mr. Darcy, what say you that we defer this discussion for another time, as we are now in this beautiful ballroom with all eyes upon us? Surely, you would not wish to add jealous husband to your list of eminent qualities."

"No more than you would wish to add capricious wife to yours, my love," he uttered daringly. "Shall we dance, Mrs. Darcy?"

"By all means, Mr. Darcy," Elizabeth voiced with an offer of her hand.

It was an exceedingly long evening. The unsurprisingly quiet carriage ride home seemed an eternity.

Darcy felt he had waited long enough for his wife to join him in bed. He went to Elizabeth's dressing room. Despite the lateness of the hour, he found her with her lady's maid, Hannah, who was assisting her out of her gown.

"Please leave us," he said.

Upon her maid's quick exit, Elizabeth turned to Darcy. "What was that all about?"

"Her services are no longer required for the evening. I should like to attend to you myself…, if that is quite all right with you, madam."

"As I will need help in removing this gown, and you have been as presumptuous as to dismiss my maid. I find I have no choice."

"Please tell me, what is the matter? You barely have spoken a civil word to me all evening."

"Oh well, you know me, ever the capricious wife."

"Is that what is bothering you? I meant nothing by that remark."

"Of course you did not."

Sweeping her hair aside, Darcy leaned forward to brush his lips along the back of her neck. "Truly, I did not. It was merely a response to you accusing me of jealousy, which of course I am. I hated seeing all the attention those men lavished upon you all evening," he confessed as he started to undo the tiny silk-covered buttons of her gown.

"As the Season has hardly even begun, I suggest you endeavour to find a way to accustom yourself to any attentions that I might receive. I can see that I will certainly have to, as regards you."

"Why should you ever feel jealousy, my love? You know that I only have eyes for you."

"Yes, of course." *And apparently anyone who happens to bear a strong resemblance to me,* she did not voice aloud. As Elizabeth was now able to tend to herself, she stepped away from Darcy. "Thank you for your assistance—I can manage on my own from here."

Darcy was discouraged. "Then I shall wait for you in my bed..., you will join me," he stated with some degree of uncertainty.

"I will be along shortly."

After a quarter-hour or so, Elizabeth finally made her way into Darcy's room. He was sitting up in bed anticipating her arrival. He graced her with a gorgeous smile. One she did not return as she parted the covers and got into bed. When Darcy moved to her side of the bed to embrace her, Elizabeth stalled his efforts, "I am afraid I am very tired after such a long evening. I bid you goodnight."

Darcy was frustrated thoroughly. He had watched her the whole night as she graced the ballroom floor, and the entire time he envisioned how it would be to make love to her once they returned home. Nothing turned out as he had planned.

~ ~ ~

Tattersail was extremely proud of himself. He could imagine no sweeter revenge than observing the tension between the newlyweds upon their departure from the ball. *If only, I had thought to speak with Mrs. Elizabeth Darcy when she was in his highness's service...* A pointless conjecture on his part, he considered. That Fitzwilliam Darcy married his former employee sent shock throughout the *ton*. No one could have imagined. No, informing the unsuspecting wife of his foe as he did was a stroke of genius.

Sir Tattersail considered the proud and haughty young master of Pemberley a bitter enemy—to a greater extent than even Darcy himself was aware. Tattersail cared even less for Colonel Richard Fitzwilliam than he did for Darcy. For years, he observed the two of them in their callous treatment of the eager mamas and young women of the *ton*. "Two rich and spoilt cads" was how he characterised them.

Tattersail's family had all the rank and none of the privileges of elite society. His father died whilst he was but a small lad, leaving his mother to raise his younger sister and him as best she could. As fate would have it, his sister enjoyed a close friendship with Miss Mary Dupree. Miss Dupree was a wealthy gentleman's daughter. Her fortune of 40,000 pounds aside, Tattersail thought himself in love with the young heiress. Although always managing to be in her company, under the guise of spending time with his sister, he remained the consummate gentleman. He anxiously awaited her coming-out Season. He was sure she had grown quite fond of him and would welcome his suit.

Her parents had other plans for their daughter's future. Mrs. Dupree shared a common acquaintance with Lady Matlock—one she used to her advantage to put her daughter in the path of Mr. Fitzwilliam Darcy. Poor Miss Dupree soon found herself quite caught-up in Darcy and Richard's game. Showered with attention from Darcy, during their first meeting, the innocent young maiden easily persuaded herself that she was in love.

"Miss Dupree," he recalled his ardent plea some four years earlier, "you must not allow yourself to be persuaded that Fitzwilliam Darcy cares for you."

"That is where you are mistaken. If you could but have seen how he looked at me," the besotted young woman waxed poetically, "how he spoke with me throughout the evening, and how attentive he was to my every need."

"But, that is just it. I have seen him do the same thing on so many other occasions, with so many other young ladies such as you. It is all a game to him. He does not care for you. He is as heartless as he is haughty."

"I think you are simply jealous. Yes, that is it. You are jealous that he has managed to endear himself towards me in one evening in such a way that you have been unable to carry out in all the years I have known you."

"I have endeavoured to show you the respect you deserve. I honour you, while HE toys with you."

"You are quite mistaken. I will be the mistress of Pemberley before the end of summer. You shall see."

The next weeks of Mr. Darcy's neglect and inattention left Miss Dupree broken-hearted and disillusioned. Indeed, Tattersail did his best to recover her spirits during that time. He failed miserably. She spurned his advances and rejected his proposal in such a hateful and cruel manner that any love or compassion he once felt for her all but disappeared. Never again would he suffer such an indignity. Two years passed before he reconsidered his stance and decided that indeed, he would offer for her once more. Still discouraged and somewhat depressed, Miss Mary Dupree accepted the hand of a gentleman twice her age. Sir Tattersail missed his chance to marry a woman he cared for—a woman with a fortune that might have set his family up quite nicely.

He blamed Darcy for his loss. He blamed Richard. He hated them even more as he continued to witness the pattern of behaviour exhibited towards Miss Dupree played out time and again with other young women.

That was over four years earlier. Yet, Sir Tattersail recalled the pain of that time as clearly as if it had occurred the day before. *Revenge—how sweet the taste.*

~ Chapter 7 ~
Much like Fencing

Several days had passed. The atmosphere continued to be rather chilly between Mr. and Mrs. Darcy. Elizabeth had yet to decide how to deal with Sir Tattersail's speech, and Darcy was unwilling to apologise for that which he had not been confronted.

Elizabeth had been forced to deal with the awareness of gentlemen's indiscretions before. Lord Robert, Lady Ellen's eldest son, made no secret of the fact that he kept a mistress. Elizabeth had seen the woman in Lord Robert's company at the theatre on more than one occasion. She often wondered during such times what it must be like for Lady Elise to live with the knowledge of her husband's infidelity. Elizabeth questioned if she could bear to be one of those wives, who, along with society, turned a blind eye to said proclivities. *Is my own husband as callous as that? I must know.*

Later that day, Elizabeth and Darcy were together in the library. Elizabeth had stared at the same page in her book for a while. She silently debated whether the time was right to confront Darcy, for she had every intention of doing just that. Still, she had refrained from bringing up the unpleasant subject for days. Normally, she read her book with her bare feet resting in his lap, as he absent-mindedly massaged them from time to time, while reading his own book. Not that day. Elizabeth and Darcy were situated on either side of the sofa with as much distance between them as possible.

At length, she set her book aside and positioned herself to face his direction.

"William, Sir Tattersail said that you kept a woman for years. Is that true?"

Even without knowing beforehand what exactly Tattersail may have told his wife, Darcy had been dreading the ensuing conversation, nonetheless. At least now that she had finally voiced her concerns, Darcy knew what he was up against. Of course, he had not expected her to be that direct.

He observed that she did not seem upset, at least not out-wardly. The voice of caution pervaded his innermost thoughts. He started to wonder why she had waited so long to share her conversation with Tattersail. He gazed at her in an uncommitted fashion. Perhaps, it was a conversation that she did not wish to have—it was certainly that way for him.

"I am sorry?" Darcy attempted to stall for time.

"Is it true that you kept a woman for years?" Elizabeth re-peated her question in the same tone as before.

"Kept a woman—I would say that is not true, certainly not in practice."

"How am I to understand you? Do you suggest that you kept a woman in spirit?"

"Elizabeth, I never kept a woman."

"Then, why would anyone accuse you thus?"

The conversation was not going to be as easy as he had supposed, for now she clearly was upset. He thought that perhaps he might deflect her ire with idle questions till she calmed a bit, thereby allowing for a rational discussion.

"Elizabeth, how am I to ascertain the motives of my detractors?"

"Are you suggesting that the gentleman was lying, Mr. Darcy? Should another one of your detractors approach me with a similar tale, should I believe that he or she is a liar as well?"

Darcy mentally calculated the odds that someone else might approach her in that regard. There was no point in further delaying the inevitable.

Abashedly, he finally held her gaze and awkwardly admitted, "There was a particular woman in an establishment that I patronised long ago, mind you, with whom I had an exclusive arrangement."

"How could you do such a thing?" Her voice weighed heavily with heart-wrenching agony that could hardly be disguised.

"Elizabeth, what has that to do with our lives? It is part of my past. All that really matters is the two of us…, here and now."

"Yet, I was told the woman bore a strong resemblance to me! You are absolutely despicable."

Darcy reached for Elizabeth's hand. Amidst her resistance, he covered her hand with his own. "I never wish to be lowered in your esteem, my love. I implore you to be sensible in your judgement of my past indiscretions, if you will, prior to the forming of an understanding between us and long before I had any reasonable hope for a future between us.

"You knew full well that I had sworn off marriage, did you think that I had also taken a vow of celibacy?"

She withdrew her hand forcefully. "I do not know what to think! That you shared yourself so willingly with another, I find quite perplexing."

"This is hardly an excuse, I know. In truth, it meant nothing. It was purely physical, much like fencing."

Elizabeth jumped from the sofa and faced him directly. "THAT, if I recall correctly, was a part of your daily routine!"

Fencing! Why did I say that? What an outrageous comparison! Now every time I head off to fencing practice, this ridiculous conversation will come to mind. Changing tactics once more, Darcy abruptly closed his book, and stood directly before her, causing her to strain her neck upwards to continue to hold his gaze.

"Elizabeth, I will not be chastised any further on this matter. I ended it long before I formed any serious intentions towards you. I ask that you consider it a matter settled." Darcy kissed her upon her forehead and exited the room, leaving Elizabeth to stew.

And stew she did. Elizabeth was incensed! She looked about wishing for something that she might toss to vent her frustration, when she espied the book he so abruptly cast aside. It was one of his favourites—a precious and highly prized possession. *What if some unfortunate fate should befall it,* she wondered. *Would he then think before summarily dismissing me again?*

Of course, Elizabeth would never actually do such a thing. Her love for books was as great as his. However, she determined that he had not heard the last of the matter. *How dare he dismiss my concerns so casually?*

~ ~ ~

He found himself in a place in which he rarely ventured since his return to town. Even with Jane in residence and as such, often in the company of his wife, Darcy contented himself to remain at home all throughout the day in contrast to whiling the hours away at White's. As he walked into the club and looked around, he was not the least bit surprised to see all the old, familiar faces languishing about. Darcy threw himself down in a fine leather chair beside Richard's.

"I need a drink."

"You have come to the right place, old man." Richard signalled for the server. Upon placing two drink orders, one for Darcy and one for himself, he returned his attention to his cousin. "How *is* your lovely wife?"

"Do not ask."

"The honeymoon is over—aye."

"Not if I can help it."

"Then what in Heaven are you doing here and drinking at this hour?"

Exactly! Darcy knew that he should have stayed and continued the conversation with Elizabeth, but what would have been the point? Why subject himself to his wife's ire when he had done absolutely nothing wrong—at least, not according to his way of thinking.

Richard continued, "You will let me know if there is anything that I can do. Perhaps you might tell me what the matter with your wife is this time."

"Nothing that a little time and space will not heal," Darcy responded. "Actually, I have a more pressing matter to discuss as regards an old acquaintance of ours, one who seems hell-bent on causing trouble."

"And who might that be?"

"Sir Walter Tattersail."

"That old fellow—what has he done?"

"He has taken it upon himself to inform my wife of my past follies with a certain courtesan."

"My, my, my...that is, indeed, cause for concern. What do you intend to do about it?"

"I have yet to decide, but I am a firm believer that such an act should not go unnoticed."

"Be careful, my friend. Elizabeth knows of your past; no greater harm can come from it all now. You have told her everything, have you not?"

"Well, I have not told her everything, not exactly. Besides, it is not that I object to Elizabeth finding out about my past. It is more than that. I take an exception to men approaching her on such a familiar basis."

"She is a beautiful woman. She is lively and charismatic. Both, men and women, alike, will be drawn to her. I suggest you get used to people seeking her acquaintance; even other gentleman. The only alternative is to keep her hidden away in Derbyshire. Now, I ask you my friend, how likely is that?"

Darcy's spirits began to rise a bit in Richard's company. He chuckled as he considered his cousin's last words. *Hide my wife off in Derbyshire to keep her from other men; not terribly likely indeed.* "I have no objection to others admiring her from afar, but to approach Mrs. Darcy so familiarly. It gives me great cause for concern."

"See here, I am not at all opposed to seeing Tattersail get his comeuppance for his interference. I am not disinclined to exact my own brand of punishment on your behalf. However, the best defence you can offer to your wife against future offences is full knowledge of the truth."

Whether he would admit it or not, Darcy knew that he could always count on Richard. After rounding off several drinks with his cousin, Darcy returned to his home and headed straight for his study. He had much to contemplate. As an adult,

Darcy had never answered to anyone for his actions. Why then should he have considered that he might have to answer for them in the future; to a wife who was not even a faint inclination, to someone whom he could not even conceptualise at the time?

The truth was he had never considered it even after meeting Elizabeth and bringing her into his home, so convinced was he that he would never marry her…, could never marry her.

In all his adult life, he had never loved anyone but Elizabeth. He had never known anyone like her. Even the physical pleasures that he experienced with her were beyond a doubt the most intensely gratifying of his life. Not that he actually compared. Though he may have thought of her when in flagrante delicto with another, once he savoured the pleasure of his lips upon her delicate skin, he never thought of any woman, but her, ever again.

As he considered his conversation with Richard, he had to admit to the soundness of his advice. He had not handled the talk with his wife properly. He had to approach the next conversation differently. Darcy would endeavour to be contrite. His wife's good opinion was paramount.

He would not allow her to suffer over his past, even if he believed she was being unreasonable. She was his wife. It was his mission to be mindful of her sensibilities. It was understandable that she felt hurt by the sudden awareness of his past. He decided to go to her and to apologise in whatever fashion it would take to soothe her.

In the solitude of her sitting-room, Elizabeth gave the matter some thought, as well. *Of course, there had been other women before me. No doubt, he is well versed in such matters.* The gentle manner in which he had initiated her to their marriage bed was evidence of that. She recalled thinking even then, that such prowess could not have been obtained solely through the extensive reading of books. He knew everything about her body, more than even she could conceive, and he never failed to satisfy her.

Was it simply too easy not to consider just how that came about? To consider that, all evidence to the contrary, she was the only woman he had ever known in that way, just as he was the only man for her. Elizabeth was far too sensible to pretend unawareness of the double standard for young men and young women. A gentleman's sexual proclivities, both in and outside of wedlock, were just that, but such conduct in a woman characterised her for life.

She considered, *Surely, I must allow that it is a part of his past and not who he is now.*

She asked herself what it would take for her to put the matter out of her mind altogether, and move forward. Did she need to know details? How many? Where? When? Why? Perchance there had been assignations with women whom she might encounter, at some point in life. If such were the case, certainly, she would need to know, would she not? She felt vulnerable enough to the viciousness of the women of the *ton,* who sought but could not have him, who thought she was not good enough for him, and made no secret of their disdain. If she should learn that one or more of said women had indeed been his lover, had shared his bed, how then might she feel?

They met each other halfway.

"Elizabeth, I was wrong to be so short with you. You are my wife, my life. I apologise for my inconsideration earlier. You have a right to be upset by what you heard, and every right to ask questions of my past. You must know how much I love you. I have no wish for secrets between us.

"The woman from my past, whom Sir Tattersail spoke of, meant nothing to me. When I knew I loved you, once our intimacy warranted us as more than close friends that became meaningless to me. I abandoned that lifestyle long before I ever even knew you cared for me. I have no excuse for my poor judgement. Certainly, it was not my intention to hurt you."

"Mr. Darcy, I have given this matter some thought. You must not believe that I am naïve. Of course, it was a shock to be confronted with gossip about your past from a stranger, but I accept it as just that, your past. I lived with you long enough to know that you were far from perfect. Through the strength of your love for me, I was able to look beyond that and accept you as you are, just as you accepted me. I love you. I will not judge you."

Elizabeth raised her hand in a refusal of Darcy's embrace. *Does he honestly think it will be as easy as that?* She continued, "That said, I do not want to be caught off guard by accusations against you again. Tell me now, have I reason for concern? Am I likely to meet any of your sexual conquests, here in town, in Derbyshire or anywhere, for that matter?"

"I have never had a *relationship* of any kind, with any women other than those at Madam Adele's. It is my most ardent wish that you should never meet a woman of that class, under any circumstances."

"How long did this go on?"

"What? My association with Madam Adele's? For years, Elizabeth. It was—it IS deemed an acceptable practice for young men of my station in life."

"I find this all too astounding. I lived under the same roof with you, and yet I feel that I did not even know you at the time."

"You know me now, Elizabeth. You know that I love you."

"I realise that this is not uncommon in your world. Still, I find it deplorable."

"In retrospect, I know it was reprehensible that I participated in any of that and that I kept up such associations. Knowing now as I do, how this has affected you, do you doubt that I would not change every aspect of that part of my life, if I could?"

"She looked just like me," her voice trailed off in despair. "How could you not but compare?" Elizabeth asked in a whispered voice, breaking eye contact with him.

"I have never even thought of another woman, since I have been with you. I love you. No one compares to you," he spoke to her gently, lifting her chin to look into her eyes. Eyes cast with wary.

"I suppose that is a small consolation."

It seemed the unease would last a while longer. Elizabeth would not judge her husband, which was not to say that she would not stand to see him suffer a bit more for his prior indifference.

~ ~ ~

Several days later...

She slept on her stomach, her arms resting underneath her plush pillow. With her face turned away, all that could be seen was her long, beautiful hair cascading off to the side.

A space between them of several feet, though atypical, was easily redressed. He pulled the covers back and revealed her exquisite nakedness. At least that was something—but why the temptation? Why taunt?

Their agreement never to sleep under the same roof apart from one another was adhered to the letter, but hardly in the spirit in which Darcy had hoped. It had been far too many nights by his count. A smile and a light kiss good-night were always followed by the view of her back.

He brushed her hair aside revealing her neckline. It was smooth to his touch, with a taste of heaven. Her earlobe was divine, especially the sweet spot just behind.

The soft, delicate length of her spine was sensuously pleasing, as well. Powerfully aroused; he gently caressed her slender waistline as he pressed against her.

His decidedly headstrong wife—*she cannot be yet asleep.*

He lavished soft kisses down her back, with tender caresses along her side, the smooth silkiness of him pressing against her from behind, between her shapely thighs. *When has this ever failed to rouse her?*

At last, she sighed deeply. She then lay on her back with both hands resting upon her pillow, on either side of her head. Her knees bent slightly as her legs relaxed invitingly. She did not open her eyes. Her mouth seemed less under her control as her eager lips parted slightly. Her beautiful bosom, both treasured and adored, was her ultimate betrayal.

The touch of his fingers upon her lips was similarly felt along and around her breasts and her navel. He trailed his fingers lower and lower, until they rested in a moist pool. He needed her beyond measure.

The deep, sensual tone of his voice beckoning, "Elizabeth, look at me," was met with no response. Having come too far to stop but willing to, should her stubbornness persist, he made a final silent plea.

His fingers were replaced by his lips, trailing the corners of her mouth, her neckline and shoulders. Soft tugging of her taunt nipples unleashed her moans. Such sweet sounds drew his eyes to her face, her amazing eyes. He kissed her lips with tremendous enthusiasm and coupled with her at once.

She met his pace and devoured his passionate kisses. Sounds of love reached a resounding crescendo, at length replaced by rapidly paced heartbeats.

He smiled and looked deeply into her eyes, "Good morning, Mrs. Darcy."

~ ~ ~

The Darcys had heard nothing from Lady Catherine de Bourgh since she wrote to her nephew soon after their return to Pemberley from their honeymoon journey. Her sole purpose in writing was to rebuke him for his fool-hearty choice of a bride. Her bitter sounding words practically exploded from the page...,

You can be at no loss, nephew, to understand the depths of my despair. Your own heart, your own conscience, must tell you of my shock and astonishment. To deny your late mother her favourite wish, to turn your back on honour, decorum, prudence, and even interest, to reject the splendid fortune of Rosings Park, what in heaven's name were you thinking?

Let me assure you, nephew, my dear sister would be most aggrieved and disappointed in your choice of a pretentious country upstart without family, connections, or fortune as the mistress of Pemberley.

How is this to be endured? I am most seriously displeased!

Fortunately, she made no further attempt to venture to Pemberley after her mission to carry her point with Lord and Lady Matlock failed to go liked she planned. They turned the tables on her by threatening that she would be the one to face the family's censure should she cast dispersions upon Darcy and his bride.

Once again, Darcy was in receipt of a letter from her Ladyship. She wrote to tell him of her intention to receive him during Easter, in keeping with their yearly tradition, as if there had never been a breach between them. The only sign that she was in acceptance of his changed familial status was reflected in a post-script to her letter.

Bring your wife, if you must.

~ *Chapter 8* ~
Two for Two

For Darcy to ignore his aunt's invitation and in so doing, abandon what had been a long-standing act of his duty to his family, surely would be interpreted as some malice on his wife's part. Elizabeth was in every way agreeable that he should suffer no further breach in his family on account of their marriage. Nevertheless, what with her Ladyship's *warm* invitation, Elizabeth was not inclined to accompany her husband. It was an annual trip, after all, where both Darcy and Richard were expected. If Elizabeth accompanied her husband, it would mean that Jane must accompany them, as well. The last thing Elizabeth wanted was to throw Jane and Richard in the same company for an extended visit to Kent.

The timing of the visit was in every way bad. Darcy was reluctant to make the trip at all, if it meant that he would be parted from his wife. Elizabeth and he had yet to regain the former level of connubial bliss as shared before she learned the facts of his past. *Surely, a long leave-taking at this time is not in our best interests*, he considered. Elizabeth did not share his sentiments. She insisted that he go. He needed to heal the rift with his aunt. She would stay in town with her sister, and endeavour to spend more time with her own aunt and uncle in Darcy's absence.

The carriage ride to Kent was by far one of the most tedious the two gentlemen ever recalled. One was intent upon gazing out of the window with a look of utter forlorn. The other had no choice but to endure the occasional discontented sighs. Darcy and he nearly arrived in Kent, before Richard made any attempt to prod him from his sombre mood.

"It pains me to see you go on so stupidly," Richard spoke in a disgusted manner.

"I beg your pardon?" Darcy asked, his reverie effectively broken.

"Look at yourself—behaving as a lovesick fool. One would think that the two of you have never been apart!"

"We have not been apart, not since our wedding."

"It was bound to occur sooner or later. I must admit that even I did not expect it would be as soon as this trip. I was quite looking forward to the company of the ladies."

"I have no doubt. Elizabeth was not inclined to join me on this trip for that very reason."

"You mean to say that your wife continues to doubt my intentions towards Mrs. Eliot."

"I shall not lay the blame entirely upon your cavalier behaviour towards my sister. It is more than that—actually. Elizabeth is not reconciled to my past—not entirely."

"Continuing troubles in paradise, I see. There are few gentlemen in your position who would tolerate such grief," Richard chided.

"Spoken like a man who has never been in love."

"Your point is well taken!"

"At any rate, I am inclined to wrap up Lady Catherine's affairs as soon as can be. I wish to return to town as quickly as possible."

"I am all for that. This reminds me, as regards our old friend Tattersail, and his loose lips; you need not concern yourself on that score any longer."

"How is that?"

"Believe me, my friend; you do not want to know."

"Richard!"

"Trust me on this. Everything has been dealt with—even within the law," he said, while thinking, *just barely.* "He shall not be a problem for you or your wife again."

Both gentlemen leaned back with their arms folded and their legs resting on the opposite seat. Darcy returned once again to his private musings.

Richard silently recalled just how he had dealt with Tattersail. It turned out that the old fellow was nowhere near as honourable as he would have others believe. He too suffered sins of the flesh, but on a far greater scale than either Darcy or Richard might have conceived, for he had entangled himself with the wife of a prominent Member of Parliament. Richard, of course, knew the man personally, as well as by reputation. He was rumoured to have been complicit in the untimely death of one of his wife's unfortunate paramours. Power and influence were enough to quell such speculations. Indeed, he was an extremely jealous husband who did not take kindly to the notion of being branded a cuckold.

The Fitzwilliam family belonged in the same sphere as the prominent politician; it was not too hard for Richard to flush out rumours of Tattersail's dalliance with the man's wayward wife. Although, she was guarded in her personal affairs, she suffered another vice that Richard could exploit. She had a fierce gambling habit and had managed to go deeply into debt. Yes, her husband was rich and powerful; but he was far more miserly than he was jealous. She knew not what to do.

Richard managed the situation to acquire as much of her debts as would be needed to force her hand. He offered to forgive her debt. In return, she must do something for him.

Not only was the woman scandalous in her vices, she was also remarkably beautiful. She thought that Colonel Richard Fitzwilliam might only be interested in sharing her bed. Richard let her know in no uncertain terms that he wanted something far more valuable than an illicit liaison. He wanted proof, of what was vaguely speculated, that Sir Tattersail was her lover. Knowing what it would mean to surrender such proof, but equally worried what it might mean to have her massive gambling debts exposed, she offered up the proof, in the form of handwritten letters from Sir Tattersail himself.

Though that was all that Richard needed to persuade Tattersail never to interfere in the Darcys' lives again, he left the gentleman with a not so gentle physical reminder as well—one that rendered him speechless for a spell.

The carriage rolled on and soon they arrived at Rosings Park. Darcy and Richard quickly descended. Darcy stretched as he looked about the immaculately groomed grounds. "Let us get this over."

~ ~ ~

Lady Catherine de Bourgh was most anxious to receive the Darcys at Rosings, in spite of her less than cordial invitation to Mrs. Darcy. She was sure that if Darcy's wife understood her place, she would be grateful for the opportunity to visit Rosings Park. Darcy had not prepared his aunt for his wife's absence, hoping till the very end that she would agree to accompany him.

Sitting in her elegant chair, assuming a regal stance, as if perched upon a throne, her Ladyship was confounded when her nephews entered the drawing-room alone. "Darcy, what is the meaning of this? Where is your wife?"

"I beg your pardon, Madam. Mrs. Darcy did not accompany me," he declared.

"How dare she dismiss any invitation that I deign to extend to her? Does she not recognise the honour that I have bestowed?

"Why, she did not have the decency to express her regrets —rather she simply chose to dismiss my invitation out of hand? This is not to be borne."

"Mrs. Darcy sends her regrets Lady Catherine, and she sends you this letter, which I have been charged to present to you personally."

He handed his aunt the note. She hastily tore open the seal and perused its contents.

Lady Catherine,
   I have decided against being brought along by my husband. I choose to honour a prior commitment.

Mrs. Darcy

"Why—I never heard of such a thing! What on earth is the meaning of this, nephew? What sort of commitment detains her in town?"

"My wife's sister is visiting from Hertfordshire. Their plans were fixed before we received your invitation."

"A poor excuse at best. Does she not realise that you visit Rosings Park every year at Easter? Surely she does not make plans without first consulting you." Lady Catherine went on and on complaining of the injustice of Elizabeth's slight. It was not so much that she wanted Elizabeth to join Darcy. What she wanted most anxiously was to put the new Mrs. Darcy in her place. To have her plans thwarted in such a way, vexed her exceedingly.

Darcy took the first available opportunity to escape his aunt's company. He wanted to get started as soon as possible. He did not intend to stay in Kent, a day longer than necessary.

Nestled away in the study at Rosings Park, Darcy exhaled noisily at the mounds of unsettled estate business before him. He began to consider that Lady Catherine had deliberately allowed her affairs to remain in such a state as an excuse to keep him there as long as possible. He sighed. He was in for a long visit.

As was his wont during such visits, Darcy buried himself in his tasks, only allowing for meals and the obligatory evening routine. Richard was left with the onerous task of entertaining his aunt and his cousin Anne. Lady Catherine soon took to the habit of eyeing her second favourite nephew with an odd mixture of curiosity and regard that he had, theretofore, never experienced on any of his previous visits. Knowing his aunt as he did, he could only imagine what she might be up to.

It was not all business as usual for Darcy, however. If he did not spend half so much time as he did daydreaming of Elizabeth, he might have made a far greater dent in the piles of work before him.

He had written to Elizabeth every day since his arrival in Kent, and she had yet to respond to any of his missives. Her neglect troubled him exceedingly. He replayed their last days together over and over again—how she still seemed to be nursing hurt feelings.

Will she ever truly forgive me, or will there always be this gulf between us? Darcy thought back to the day that he asked

Elizabeth to accept his hand in marriage, and she agreed. It was not the first time he thought about that day. He did so often. He brought to mind the promises he made. One promise stood out amongst the rest. She demanded that he not hurt her again, as he had in making the preposterous secret benefactor proposal— in failing to consider the implications of his offer. He said that he would do everything in his power never to hurt her again.

Had he done everything in his power not to hurt her? They were only beginning to learn to live together as one; mistakes were bound to be made. Of course, there were things he might have done differently. One would have been to be completely forthcoming when she initially questioned him on Tattersail's accusations, but there was no guarantee that it would have made a difference. After he had told her the whole story, it had a seemingly little effect upon her acceptance. Of that, Darcy utterly was convinced.

He recalled his promise to be a deeply devoted husband, a generous lover, and a most loyal friend. Darcy felt that he was all those things. He loved her more than anything or anyone else in the world. He told her so, almost every day. At times, he might have failed to consider that it was a trial for Elizabeth to accustom herself to her life as Mrs. Darcy. It was often a trial for him to acclimate to his role as her husband. Both were in an unfamiliar territory. While he conceded to himself that, upon occasion, he took her for granted; he quickly acknowledged that she likely took him for granted, as well.

That he was a generous lover was of no doubt in his mind. His need for her was so great; it was as though he was addicted to her. He always put her pleasure before his own and as far as he could tell, she could have no cause to repine. *Two for two*, Darcy thought.

He was even convinced of his loyalty to her as a friend. For as long as he remembered, his friendship with Richard was the closest and most enduring he had ever known. That is till he met Elizabeth. Though he had not tossed Richard aside entirely, nor would he ever, he had surely done all that he could in showing her that she was far more significant to him than Richard could ever be.

Rather than rack his brain trying to figure out what he had done to cause his wife repeatedly to ignore his letters, he decided he would write to her once more, to let her know how her silence was distressing him.

~ ~ ~

Jane had received a letter from her husband that morning. While sitting at the breakfast table as she read, she shared a few snippets with Elizabeth.

"He writes to say that the girls remain with their grandparents." She read some more. "His arrival is delayed once again." In the letter, Jane was encouraged to remain in town and enjoy her time with her sister. And, so it was. Jane put the letter aside as she raised her cup to her lips to sip her tea. She seemed, to her sister, completely unaffected by the news.

Having received another missive from Darcy, Elizabeth too perused the contents of her letter. She read silently.

Dearest Elizabeth,

You have yet to respond to any of my letters. Your silence pains me immensely. I realise that I made a mistake—I apologised for that, and yet you have not forgiven me. You choose to believe that I have betrayed you—betrayed our love.

Elizabeth was so taken aback by the reproachful tone of her husband's letter that she read the opening paragraph once more. *Is he blaming me for all this?* Flabbergasted, she read his unsparing words for a third time.

Jane observed her sister's confounded behaviour. With no idea at all what exactly Darcy had conveyed she sought to question Elizabeth. "Does he say when the Colonel and he are to return to town?" Alas, Jane had asked Elizabeth the same question on more than one occasion over the past week.

Caught off guard by Darcy's letter, on the one hand, and frustrated by her sister's ostensible fixation upon Richard's plans, on the other, Elizabeth was no longer able to contain her sentiments. "Excuse me Jane, but you seem far more concerned over Richard's return to town, than you do your own husband's."

"Lizzy, you know that is not fair."

"Fair? What has fairness to do with this?"

"Of course, fairness has nothing at all to do with any of this," Jane stated. "Perhaps the better sentiment would have been that you are far too judgemental and apt to believe that which you choose to believe in this matter.

"You are so convinced of your own opinion on this, as well as every other matter involving my life, that you fail to consider that you might be mistaken."

"Jane, how can I allow myself to be mistaken when all the evidence supports my contention? Your eager response to Richard's attentions leaves me with no doubt."

"Can you not even allow yourself to be wrong in this matter?"

"No—not when I know that I am right," Elizabeth expressed with utter conviction.

"Just as you insisted that Mr. Bingley was deeply attached to me, despite my words to the contrary—now you insist upon believing that there is something untoward between the Colonel and myself, in spite of my repeated assertions that we are simply friends. Must everything always be as you would believe it to be? Always conforming to what you believe to be right or wrong? What is and what is not?"

Jane was upset! "It is so like you, Lizzy, in believing yourself to be always right and anyone who does not share your sentiments to be always wrong. You have forever been too fond of your own judgements and opinions and looked askance towards those who would disagree. Why, even your husband does not escape your censure! You are determined to make him suffer for acts committed long before you exchanged your wedding vows, because you do not believe his apology to be based upon true remorse."

Yes, it appeared Elizabeth had shared that intimate knowledge with her sister. "You even supposed that Mr. Darcy should turn his back against his family, even though they have embraced you wholeheartedly, simply because they will not give up on the tenets that they have espoused their entire lifetime!"

Jane was on a roll, fuelled by anger or jealousy, it did not really matter for she truly believed that Elizabeth needed to hear the things she was saying. "You are quite hypocritical in that. You insist that the Fitzwilliams do not look down upon your family, when you do so yourself!"

"How do you presume such a thing?" Elizabeth rejoined angrily.

"You know full well that Mr. Collins and my mother wished to be here for the Season, and you have yet to extend an invitation to them. Are you afraid that they will embarrass you? Nevertheless, you would scorn Lady Ellen for sharing a similar sentiment towards those whom you deem to be worthy."

"Now, YOU are not being fair!" Elizabeth accused her sister in an astonished tone.

"It is my turn to ask you—what has fairness to do with this? It pains me to say these things to you Lizzy, but I feel you must hear them. Contrary to your opinion, the world does not revolve around Mrs. Elizabeth Darcy!"

Elizabeth attempted to regain her composure after suffering momentary confusion on receiving such a direct and in her estimation, wholly unwarranted reproach. "You have said quite enough, Jane! I had no idea you felt as strongly as you do on these matters. Whatever I have done to incite such anger, I am most apologetic. If you will excuse me now, I have a household to manage!"

Elizabeth picked up her letter and before quitting the room, turned to her sister. "Should you wish to apologise for this unseemly outburst, I shall be in my sitting-room."

Elizabeth passed more than a few hours alone in her sitting-room. She tried her best to focus her attention upon her household accounts. She could not. The tumult of her mind was painfully great.

Is this really her opinion of me? My own sister, how long has she felt this way? Is it jealousy? I would never have imagined Jane as capable of that. Dear, sweet Jane, what misfortune has befallen her that she should accuse me so unjustly?

Elizabeth began to consider that Jane had never been jealous of anyone. She simply was incapable of such a petty emotion. Jane, who had always had more goodness than anyone else she knew. It was only during the late hours of the afternoon that she forced herself to consider the truth of her sister's words; at least the possibility that some of what all she said might have merit.

Elizabeth recalled her husband's admonitions that she risked alienating Jane should she persist in her unkind views of her friendship with Richard. *Has it come to that? Have I alienated my own sister?*

She recalled Jane's assertion that she had been too hard on her husband, causing him to suffer needlessly by her actions. Elizabeth could not deny that she encouraged him to go to Kent…, even to go without her. She believed she was doing the right thing. He needed to mend fences with his aunt. They all could benefit from the separation, especially Jane and Richard, she thought.

Some hours later, Elizabeth remained by herself. Jane had not ventured forth to apologise for her tirade. Neither had Elizabeth sought to atone for her share of the blame. Elizabeth felt utterly and completely alone. She had not felt that way since before her marriage. Her thoughts returned to her husband's letter. She had yet to resume reading it. Feeling she might as well hear him out too, she continued reading where she left off earlier.

I find I can hardly blame you for your reticence towards me. I blame myself. In some ways, I feel that I have failed you.

With far more distances between us now than ever before since we exchanged vows, I find I cannot help but recall the day you agreed to become my wife. I admit that I was desperate to keep you with me upon your return to Pemberley. I realise that I promised you a lot. However, I was not so desperate as to say anything that I did not mean. I was indeed ready to love you the way you should be loved, the way you needed to be loved, and the way you wanted to be loved.

Although, my actions may at times suggest otherwise, allow me to say that I am as steadfast in my commitment to those words as ever. I have made mistakes. I am apt to make mistakes in the future. That points to my imperfection as a human being. It says nothing of my feelings towards you. I love you above all else in my life.

In closing, I am reminded of another promise to you—my promise to spend each day of the rest of my life, endeavouring to be a man truly worthy of your love and affection. I ask that you be patient with me, my love. I have not yet finished.

As I am known to you and to you alone, your loving and devoted husband,

William

Too far away at Rosings Park, Darcy felt quite lonely himself. How he missed Elizabeth. He longed for her. He ached for her. Every fibre of his being screamed out for her.

Each day, he wondered if that day would be the one to bring a response from his wife. Upon receipt of an urgent express the very next day, he was beside himself with worry. When first handed the express, he immediately thought, *has something happened to Elizabeth?* Seeing that the letter indeed was from Elizabeth, did little to calm him. He tore it opened.

Her words simply read..., *I need you.*

~ *Chapter 9* ~
Renewing His Path

*T*here *she is.* Elizabeth lay asleep in his bed. A more wel-come sight, he could not have envisioned. Upon receipt of her letter, Darcy's feelings were a bitter-sweet combination of gladness and heartache. His wife needed him. But what had oc-curred to provoke such a brief and poignant sentiment, after having gone days without responding to any of his letters to her?

As soon as he arrived, he immediately went to her room. She was not there. *It is late—where else would she be?* He re-turned downstairs. She was nowhere to be found. Exhausted, he decided to clean himself up from his hastened journey before seeking her out further.

In his room, alone in his bed, was the last place he would have thought to look. The silent motion of him sitting upon his bed to admire her in peaceful slumber stirred her.

Elizabeth lifted herself up from the bed. "You came."

"Of course I came. I left Kent as soon as I received your letter."

She got out of bed, slipped on her robe, and slowly walked across the cold floor in her bare feet, towards the window. She turned to face him, but her eyes would not meet his.

"Elizabeth, what is the matter?" His comforting voice was wonderfully warm and soothing.

With her arms folded in front of her chest, hugging herself in solace, Elizabeth replied, "I am almost too ashamed to say—I feel as though I have been such a wretch." Her voice cracked as she spoke.

Darcy approached her. She seemed utterly forlorn. Never before had he seen her so distraught. He took both of her hands into his and brought them to his lips to bestow light kisses upon her palms. He looked into her eyes, "You—wretched. Impossible."

He then placed both hands about her waist, drew her close and held her for a moment. He slightly surrendered her from his tight embrace, and he trailed the back of his hands along her arms. She rested her head in the cradle of his embrace. Seeing her each morning—holding her each night. How he missed her. He showered kisses along her neckline.

Amidst his tender ministrations, she protested, her voice, slightly above a whisper, "No, not this…, just hold me."

He attempted to restrain his ardour unsuccessfully, for moments later his lips were upon her neckline once more. Elizabeth broke their embrace with a slight step back. Still, he could not cease touching her. Irresistibly drawn towards Elizabeth, he suffered an urgent need to be close to her. They rested their foreheads together for a few moments until he relinquished his touch. He realised that she needed something more from him at that moment. She needed him to listen.

"Let us have a seat and talk. What has happened to cause you such great distress, my love?" Darcy asked as he led her by the hand to the sofa, to take a seat beside him.

Elizabeth recounted the terribly harsh sentiments her sister had heaped upon her, how much it pained her—indeed both of them.

"I am sorry. I can only surmise how unpleasant it must have been for the two of you."

"Indeed, it was most unpleasant. How I wished that I had listened to you more willingly. I might have spared Jane the pain of having to say such things, and myself the pain of having to hear them."

"Hush, Elizabeth," Darcy said, placing his fingertips upon her lips. "I am sure it will be all right. It cannot be nearly as bad as you think. Your sister is not one to hold a grudge. I know if you would but meet her halfway; soon you both will put this issue behind you."

"I fear it might be too late. What if she has decided to leave town?" Elizabeth repined in a low voice.

Darcy brushed her flowing dark curls behind her ear and leaned forward to kiss her upon her forehead. "We will not let that happen."

"I sincerely hope we can convince her to stay. Though she is my sister, she is my closest friend in the world. What would I do without her love and support?"

"You will never lose your sister. Even so, you will always have me. I shall always love and support you."

"Yes, I know that is true. I love you more than you know. Can you imagine what the pain of losing you would do to me?"

"You should not imagine for one moment that such pain would not be as great for me. Have faith in me. I will always be here for you. Always." They kissed. "Of course, I will not always yield to your every whim as you well know, but I will always be here when you need me."

"But we have allowed others to come between us. What is to say that might not continue?"

"Do you speak of Richard?" Darcy asked tentatively.

"Yes, his friendship with Jane; I have allowed it to become a great distraction. You have to know it is part of the reason that I did not wish to accompany you to Rosings Park; that and…," her voice trailed off as she shifted her eyes from his face.

"And what?" Darcy gently cupped her face, returning her eyes to his.

"Jane says that I am punishing you for things that have long passed. She is right, you know. Truly, I have not learnt to let go of it all."

"Certainly not; I understand it will take time to move past those feelings completely. As long as you know that you are the only woman in the world for me, for the rest of my days, it is all that matters. I love you."

Darcy stood with Elizabeth cradled in his arms and carried her to his bed. He kissed her upon her lips before lowering her down. He began to undress her. "Let me take care of you now, as only I can. Let me soothe you and take your mind away from all the unpleasantness of the past few days."

He traced the contours of her body with his fingertips as if to recommit it to memory. He placed himself upon the bed at her feet and began kissing her, proceeding slowly upwards and pausing midway. "The longer you and I were apart, the more I longed for you," he spoke softly. Deeply satisfied with the spot he had chosen, he continued, "It has been far too long, my love. I feel as though I love you even more than ever." Renewing his path, "I have spent my every waking moment missing you, my every moment of sleep, dreaming of you. Let me make you mine once again."

Amidst increasingly mounting desire, intensifying immense pleasures, and intimate conversation, what a long and deeply satisfying night it was, for both. After several hours passed, they finally fell into a deep, restful sleep in each other's arms—relaxing more comfortably than either had for weeks.

~ ~ ~

Awakening later than usual, Elizabeth came down to breakfast. She wished to have some time with Jane, only to be told that her sister had taken one of the carriages to Cheapside. Elizabeth was beside herself with remorse and thoughts that Jane might have decided to remove herself from Darcy House, altogether.

It was very soon afterwards that Elizabeth arrived at the Gardiners' home.

Jane had been there for nearly two hours, and yet she had not spoken a word of her quarrel with her sister to her aunt. Somehow, Mrs. Gardiner knew that not all was right. Jane never visited at Cheapside, outside of the company of Elizabeth, the entire time, since she had been in town. Jane's usual calm and serene air was replaced by an agitated and uneasy state that appeared to increase with the addition of Elizabeth to their party.

After nearly a quarter of an hour of stilted conversation, the two sisters, almost at once, begged for some time alone. Both felt the greater share of the blame for what had occurred between them. Both longed to heal the rift in their relationship.

"Dearest Jane, let there be no more discussion on which of us is at fault. You are my most beloved sister. I value your good opinion. I always have."

Still, Jane had to ask, "Oh Lizzy, how can you ever forgive me for some of the things that I said?"

Elizabeth would not belabour the point. They agreed that some of the words needed to be spoken and heeded, but it must not come between them. With sincere apologies accepted on both sides, Jane agreed to come back to Darcy House to await the arrival of her husband.

In an attempt to show her sister that she indeed paid attention to her words, Elizabeth invited Richard to dine with the three of them that evening. In addition, Darcy, Elizabeth, Richard, and Jane attended the theatre that night, accompanied by the Middletons. Their party included Lady Harriette, thereby affording Richard the opportunity to appear with a beautiful woman on each arm.

~ ~ ~

With the Season well under way, the Darcys were inundated with social activities both day and night. What with Darcy's wont of only accepting invitations from the Matlocks and their closest acquaintances and now Georgiana's alliance with the Middletons, they were mostly engaged with the highest echelons of the *ton*. Of course, there were a few exceptions as both Elizabeth and Jane sought to spend as much time as their busy social calendars allowed, with the Gardiners.

Lady Ellen rarely called upon the Darcys any more, preferring instead to receive them at Matlock House. That day was an exception. Georgiana was there also. The ladies were gathered around in the drawing-room having a very pleasant visit, when another caller was announced. Suddenly, Lady Ellen was reminded of why she preferred to receive the Darcys in her home. Miss Caroline Bingley waltzed into the room.

After years of engaging Darcy's society through his friendship with her brother, at long last, she had an opportunity to mingle with his esteemed aunt in an intimate setting. Caroline found the occasion to be a real honour. She made sure that her Ladyship was aware of it as she did all she could in ingratiating herself. To Caroline's way of thinking, if the *Elizabeths* of the world impressed her Ladyship, then, she was bound to favour a young woman as polished and accomplished as she. After all, in

Caroline's estimation, it was she who had attended the best schools and personified elegance and good taste, whereas Elizabeth had lacked a formal education of any sort. Her only claim to good taste, by Caroline's observations, was that she had managed to marry Mr. Darcy. *What favour I shall receive, what excellent connections, and what doors will open to me, now that I am finally able to impress upon her Ladyship, my considerable charms and gracious air.*

Always an astute studier of people, Elizabeth derived some amusement from the interaction of the two women, or lack thereof, as regarded Lady Ellen. She noted where her own husband likely honed his haughty and aloof manner towards those he considered his inferiors. At least, her husband had displayed a willingness to change in that regard—it was plain to see that her Ladyship likely never would. That she was never so openly averse to any of Elizabeth's relatives was something. It spoke volumes of her esteem for Elizabeth.

Still, Caroline was a guest in the Darcys' home, and as such Elizabeth felt some degree of courtesy should be bestowed—if, not from her other guests, then certainly from the mistress of the house. If only Caroline would have taken the hint; no amount of kowtowing towards Lady Ellen would lift her esteem. Alas, it seemed that Caroline could not help herself. Elizabeth went out of her way to be cordial. However, Caroline returned her kindness with scarcely concealed condescension while she persisted in returning Lady Ellen's barely concealed disdain with sycophancy, ultimately leaving her Ladyship with little recourse other than to respond to her in a way that gave no one any pain but Caroline, herself.

~ ~ ~

That Season marked her third including the one of her coming-out. Lady Harriette had many potential suitors but none of them was capable of engaging her. Her parents did not seem overly concerned. As handsome and accomplished as their daughter was, and with a dowry of 50,000 pounds to boot, they were sure that when she set her heart upon marriage, there would be many offers. At the age of one and twenty, her parents were contented to allow her to enjoy her carefree youth.

Once Lady Harriette graced the ballroom with her presence, there was hardly a gentleman in the room who did not take notice of her great beauty. She had only one gentleman on her mind. She purposely made herself unavailable for the first set with her late arrival so that she would be conveniently situated to speak with him when he completed that set with his wife.

He had only parted from his wife's side for a brief moment, before he found himself face-to-face with the determined young lady. "Mr. Darcy, I believe you promised me the second set."

Darcy eyed her sceptically. She kept at it. "Come now, sir. Surely, you recall our conversation at my brother's home, last evening. You promised me the second set. I could do little else but look forward to it all day." She teasingly pouted.

Considering as he did that he rarely listened with much interest to half of what the young lady said when they were to-gether, he was pretty sure that he made no such promise. Nonetheless, willing to appease her, he consented and led her to the dance floor.

She was quite effusive, even as she spoke of matters of little to no consequence. He was her captive audience for the duration of the set. She was determined to make the most of it. Darcy had little choice but to converse with her throughout the entirety. To do otherwise would have been considered rude, and he really had no desire to give offence to the young lady so connected to his family, and thus to him.

He looked about the room at the end of the set in search of his wife. Not spotting her anywhere amongst the assemblage, he decided to step outside to escape the crowd and get a much-needed breath of fresh air. Leaning over the balcony and completely out of tune of his surroundings, he was soon joined by Lady Harriette.

"Mr. Darcy, I saw you escape the room. I could not help but follow your example. Do you mind if I join you out here?"

Darcy turned to study the young lady intently. *When did you ever require an invitation to do anything once you set your mind upon it?* "Lady Harriette, you might be mindful of the potential harm to your reputation should you be seen alone with a gentleman in this manner."

"Are we not family? Have we not spent great lengths of time in each other's company? What could be the harm in the two of us enjoying a bit of fresh air together?"

Darcy remained standing where he was, with his hands clasp behind his back as the young vixen moved closer. "This is not exactly the same as when we are together amongst family, is it?"

"I assure you that my sole purpose in following you out here is to share a breath of fresh air. You need not fear a risk of my reputation." Being almost as tall as he was, she nearly stood shoulder to shoulder with Darcy. She was about to move even closer to him when she noticed that his soul-piercing eyes were no longer fixed upon her. Instead, he looked right past her. Lady Harriette turned to follow his gaze. His eyes were settled upon his wife, who was approaching the two of them.

"Mr. Darcy, Lady Harriette," Elizabeth walked up to the two of them. "I certainly hope I am not interrupting anything." Her voice contained more annoyance than sarcasm.

"Certainly not, Mrs. Darcy, I welcome you to join us, whilst we," Darcy briefly glanced towards Lady Harriette, "enjoy the fresh air."

"Wonderful," Elizabeth said as she too stood directly before him and placed her hand lightly upon Darcy's chest—a subtle gesture on her part to encourage Lady Harriette to move along, as she was wasting her time there.

"It has been my pleasure, Mr. Darcy, but I believe I will leave you to your lovely wife. I have had enough fresh air for one evening."

Elizabeth eyed her suspiciously as she retreated. "What was that all about?"

As if completely oblivious of the situation, Darcy rejoined, "I am sorry?"

"She was standing rather close to you."

Still standing in the same spot with his hands clasped behind his back, Darcy remarked, "Was she?" He leaned forward and began kissing Elizabeth behind her ear and continued with a series of sensuous kisses along the side of her neck. "You look incredibly divine tonight." He placed his hand on the other side of her neck, lifted her face towards his and kissed her lips. "You taste wonderful."

After giving in unreservedly to his kisses, Elizabeth soon recalled herself to their surroundings. "Please, Mr. Darcy, I beg you to remember yourself," she whispered. "What if someone should happen upon us?"

With both hands gently massaging along the sides of her neck and continuing his attentions to her lips, he slowly paused. "I am sorry, my love. Let us leave this place and return to our own home at once, that I might have my way with you. I must have you."

Elizabeth broke contact with her husband. "No, I am not of a mind to leave at this moment. I would urge you to hold that thought for a few hours more."

Displeased, but in no position to do much about it, Darcy relented. "You are absolutely correct, my love. You should go back inside. I shall join you momentarily."

Elizabeth understood from his telling demeanour that it would be a while before he would be able to return to polite society.

When at last he did return to the ballroom, the physical evidence of his ardour had cooled. However, the look on his face, his alluring eyes shone smouldering fire, so much so that Elizabeth found it almost impossible to resist his silent seduction. When they danced with each other, he tended to move as close to her as the dance would permit, and he allowed his hands to linger upon hers much longer than was warranted, all the while looking at her intently. When she danced with others, he remained close by, as well.

Darcy could not wait to take his wife home. In truth, most evenings, he wished to stay at home with his wife. When out in public, he had to share her attentions with those who continued to wish to make her acquaintance. Given her personality, people were naturally drawn to Elizabeth. She made quite a favourable impression amongst the *ton* and found that she was exceedingly well received throughout.

~ ~ ~

Thomas Eliot did not covet London's society one bit. He had his fill of society during the days of his early adulthood; the exclusive gentlemen's clubs, the haves and have-nots. He stayed with his uncle and aunt (his late father's older sister) in a fairly nice neighbourhood just beyond Mayfair. His relatives were wealthy enough so that he might have a small taste of London's elite society life, but not wealthy enough that his own roots in trade on his mother's side were overlooked. Had he shared any of that aspect of his past with Jane, she might have better understood why he was in no hurry to take the Darcys up on their invitation.

Still, far too much time had passed since he last saw his wife. It was time he ventured to town to bring her home. He planned to stay on for a little stretch, a very little stretch. He, like Mr. Darcy, was a proud man. He, like Mr. Darcy, was a gentleman. The most glaring disparity between the two was that they unmistakably were not of the same sphere. Nonetheless, as a respectable gentleman, in his own right, he was not inclined to remain in town overly long, beholden to the Darcys to move about in their circle and a beneficiary of their largesse.

Nearly two full weeks had passed. Each night was filled with one sort of entertainment or another amongst London's elite; be it private balls, dining in the homes of aristocracy, or theatre in private luxury boxes. He could easily surmise that his wife was truly enjoying herself, and she seemed not at all out-of-place. He also noticed with ever-increasing concern, her rich attire. Every evening saw her in one expensive gown after another.

As in their home, they did not share an apartment. One evening when Jane took longer than expected to dress for dinner, Mr. Eliot decided to venture into her room to find out what kept her.

The knock upon her door from her husband's adjoining apartment caught Jane by surprise. It was unusual that he should wish to see her at that hour. She rose from her dressing table and strolled over to the doorway. She opened it partly, enough to espy his stern visage.

"Mr. Eliot?"

"Mrs. Eliot, do you mind if I come in?"

"You are welcome, sir," said she, as she stepped aside to allow him to pass. "Pardon me for taking as long as I have. I am nearly done. I seem to be having trouble with the clasp on this necklace."

Her husband reached his hand out to claim the piece of jewellery. "Might I assist you?"

Jane handed it to him and proceeded to watch him as he studied it intently. It was an exquisite piece. Mr. Eliot's countenance showed scarcely concealed displeasure.

"Pray tell me, you borrowed this from Mrs. Darcy."

"No, this is a gift from my sister."

"Have you made it a habit of accepting such riches?" Mr. Eliot bellowed.

Jane was taken aback by his particularly harsh tone. She said nothing. She watched as he moved towards her wardrobe. He began rummaging through the rainbow assortment of gowns with growing dismay.

"I see there are no limits to Mrs. Darcy's generosity," he said, "Jane, this is hardly proper. Surely, you must see that. I am your husband. It is I, and I alone who should provide for you."

"My sister has been kind enough to purchase a few nice things for me. Where is the harm in that?"

"Your sister? Your sister was just as penniless as you, just under a year ago!" He spoke scathingly, "It is Darcy's fortune that made this all possible. I will not have another man provide for my wife!"

Such harsh and bitter sounding words as she heard spoken from her husband's lips, were shocking! Never before had he spoken to her in such a fashion. Insulted, aggrieved, and even a bit empathetic, tears flooded her angelic eyes.

"My sister meant no harm!" Jane vehemently protested. "What should I have done? Deny her generosity. Return the gowns and thereby offend her?" She then threw herself down upon her bed and gave in to her desperate longing for a good cry.

His anger quickly gave way to confusion and guilt. He had not meant to insult her, nor had he wished to discredit her sister Elizabeth. He sat down upon the bed beside her, and attempted to soothe away her tears, with little success. Stroking her along her back, he endeavoured to correct his missteps.

"Jane, forgive me. I did not mean to sound harsh. Elizabeth is your sister. Of course, she would want to do everything in her power to bestow such generosity towards you. I am simply worried that you might be so influenced by the Darcys' lifestyle that you might tend to forget that their lifestyle is not yours. It will never be.

"Your life—our life is one of very modest and unassuming means. Tell me that you have not lost sight of that." It completely melted his heart to see his wife carry on thus. She deserved more than the coldness he had shown her. He wondered, but did not ask if she had regrets.

Slowly, her tears began to cease. She sat up and accepted the offer of his crisp white handkerchief. Jane dried her tears and blew her nose. Then, she stood and walked over to her window. She looked out onto the street below. The elegant Darcy carriage waited. The last thing Jane wanted to do at that point was to go out. She turned to face her husband. To her surprise, he stood directly behind her.

With downcast eyes, she voiced, "You have not said what I must do."

"I would only ask that you do what you feel is best."

"I think it best that I do not insult my sister," she stated. Jane did not discern any change in his countenance pursuant to her proclamation. She continued, "We are to dine at Matlock House this evening."

"Yes, I am aware of that."

"In light of your sentiments, ought we to reconsider?"

"I am only here because you are here," he took Jane's hand in his. "I beg your forgiveness for my harshness. It is just that seeing how comfortable you are amongst the Darcys' circle, caused me to fear that you might no longer be contented in mine."

"I know my place in society. Yes, everyone has been very accepting of me. I am well aware that is due solely to my connection to the Darcys and thereby Lord and Lady Matlock."

He placed his hand lovingly along her chin and lifted her face to his. "Do not underestimate yourself, Mrs. Eliot." Jane sweetly smiled in response to the inferred compliment. He continued. "Let us not keep our host and hostess any longer. The Matlocks wait."

That evening proved to be a turning point of sorts for the Eliots. Mr. Eliot saw Jane for the first time, in a long time…, not as the stepmother of his children, but as his wife. Though he could never offer her such riches as those enjoyed by her sister, he could offer her his undivided love and devotion. That night he did not return to his own apartment. He remained in Jane's bed, and he held her the entire night. He loved her as ardently as would a husband who had re-affirmed a commitment to his wife's happiness.

Days later, Elizabeth and Jane parted with no firm commitment whatsoever on when they might see each other again. An invitation to visit the Eliots in Hertfordshire was not extended. Neither had there been any mention of a return visit to Derbyshire.

As Elizabeth stood outside Darcy House with her husband and watched the carriage as it drew further away, she began to sense what Jane too had come to recognise to varying degrees, some time ago.

Their worlds were miles apart.

~ *Chapter 10* ~
Yet to Learn

In spite of the sad parting with Jane, for the first time in too many months, Darcy and Elizabeth found themselves delighted to be totally free of house-guests. Beginning with Lady Ellen's arrival in mid-November, all of Elizabeth's relatives in December, the rest of the Fitzwilliams as well as the Middletons at Christmas, Jane's extended stay, and finally Mr. Eliot's visit, the newly-wed couple scarcely had any time at all to themselves.

At last, the two could focus solely upon one another without having to accommodate the needs of family and friends. To be able to move about London, just the two of them, recalled Elizabeth to the enchanting days of their wedding journey, when Darcy and she enjoyed the vast array of diversions in Bath, Cheltenham, and Weymouth. As much as Elizabeth loved her sister, she now admitted to herself that she spent as much time with Jane over the past months as she did with her own husband. Darcy and she had not gone anywhere, together, that Jane did not go, as well.

Their time together was a balm to the Darcys' relationship. With the Season well under-way, Darcy and Elizabeth stood outside alone on the balcony of yet another of one of London's many grand homes. The moon shone bright that night. They admired its magnificence in silence.

"It is a beautiful night," Darcy eventually said to his wife, who seemed miles and miles away.

She turned to face him, "Indeed it is, my love. Though, I have to confess to a feeling that if I have been to but one of such parties as this, I have been to them all."

Darcy appreciated her sentiments. "Have you grown tired of the Season, my love?"

"I must confess to a longing for ease and freedom of life outside of London."

"So, what exactly are you saying?" He hoped she meant what he was thinking.

"I wish to go home..., to Pemberley."

~ ~ ~

The Darcys returned to Pemberley with time enough to enjoy the remnants of spring. On one particularly beautiful day, they set off on horseback for a bit of adventure. It was Elizabeth's first spring at Pemberley. The previous two years, Darcy, Georgiana, and she had spent the entire Season in London. It was as if she saw her home for the first time. The grounds, the fresh scent of late blossoming flowers, fields of bluebells as far as the eyes could see, the musical calling of birds building their nests and glimpses of natures small creatures scampering about, was in every way appealing to Elizabeth. Amazingly, Darcy and she had ridden for several hours and had managed to sustain from any overly amorous activities during their outing. They were so caught up in the many splendours of Pemberley Woods; it had been a while before they thought to return to the manor house. Fortunately, they were well equipped with food and drink for their excursion. Darcy was delighted to witness his wife's glorious discovery of Pemberley at springtime and to see their home through her eyes.

As they readied themselves for their return, Darcy mounted his own horse, effectively leaving his wife there beside her own, in much need of assistance.

"What on earth are you doing? How am I to mount Bella without your help?"

"I want you to ride with me."

"Whatever for?" she teased. Darcy coaxed her towards him by silently communicating his longing to be nearer to her in a subtle sweep of her body, a mere flickering of his soul-piercing eyes.

He reached down to lift her up. He further cajoled her to sit astride while pressing her body more closely to his own. Sitting on a horse in that manner was a first for her. The position did nothing to flatter her modesty.

"Do you not think that this position is unbecoming of the mistress of Pemberley?" she asked.

"Perhaps—but this is precisely as the master of Pemberley wishes."

Nestled behind her, Darcy wrapped his arm around her waist and brushed her hair to one side to kiss the soft skin of her neckline. The two engaged in sweet, tender kisses and caresses for a few moments before setting off at a slow, unhurried pace.

Darcy spoke softly into his wife's ear. "You know, my love, there are some things you have yet to learn about riding horseback."

"Are there? I suppose you are the only one who is capable of teaching me."

"Trust me on that, my love. Shall we commence?"

Elizabeth signalled her acquiescence with a welcoming smile. "I am in your very capable hands."

Darcy's free hand soon made way to the spot of his most ardent desire. He stroked his wife there, as his horse ambled along slowly, treating her to such pleasures as she had theretofore never experienced while riding horseback.

They eventually came upon a spot on the estate that allowed a spectacular view of the setting sun. Darcy dismounted his stallion and reached up to lift his wife down to her feet. He spread a blanket upon the ground so that they might relax and enjoy the moment. Taking a seat by her side, he promptly placed his arms around her. Comfortable in the warmth of his embrace, Elizabeth marvelled at the absolute beauty that surrounded them. The perfect culmination of the moment was the total satiation of the intense desires Darcy had unleashed within her.

~ ~ ~

The following week found Elizabeth in quite a sombre mood. Though it bothered her more than she cared to admit it, given that they had been married coming up on one full year in but a few months, that she had not yet conceived had started to take a lasting toll on her spirits. She endeavoured to keep it from her husband, just how much it had begun to distress her—he having shown no evidence of concern to her whatsoever.

The disappointment she felt every month, since she began counting was renewed once again, when she woke with the onset of her menses.

Later that same day, the two of them were outside for a picnic. Elizabeth loved picnics, most especially secluded ones with her husband. Her depressed mood seemed exacerbated. Darcy implored her to talk about what was the matter. After some urging on his part, she confided what was bothering her. Indeed, what had bothered her for many months.

Darcy endeavoured to be sympathetic. In truth, despite his obvious awareness that the heir to Pemberley had not been conceived after so many months of marriage, he had not given the matter a great deal of concern. He was pleased with the way things were, and in no hurry to change them. Nonetheless, knowing how much his wife desired children, a fact she had made known long before they confessed their love for one another, he thought better than to share those particular sentiments with her. Instead, he sought to reassure her.

"My love, you need not worry that we have yet to conceive a child. We are young still. We have plenty of time."

"I realise that perhaps I am simply being overly dramatic in this case. Nevertheless, with each month that passes by, I feel this…, emptiness."

Darcy placed his hand on her face and kissed her gently upon her lips. "I am sorry you have felt this way."

"Do not worry about me. This will pass—I am in no doubt of it. It always does." Elizabeth forced a smile to her face in trying to lighten the atmosphere.

"Still, had I known that you were suffering these feelings—I might have been able to comfort and reassure you."

"I am not convinced it would have mattered, but I thank you for your consideration, even so. Besides, it is not as though there has been a lack of trying on either of our parts."

"I am always willing to do more—much more. In fact, I recommend that we return to the house immediately, sequester ourselves in our suites, and stay in bed until we carry out our mission."

Elizabeth pretended to mull over his not so unexpected response. "I shall not argue the merits of your scheme. Indeed, I find it a very promising prospect. However, there is no need to rush off at this exact moment."

"Why waste another minute?"

"Shall I explain how this works, Mr. Darcy?" Elizabeth asked with a raised brow and a smirk. Her mood was improving steadily, with each passing moment.

Darcy's first inclination was to speak whatever was on his mind—that is, until he considered the look that graced Elizabeth's countenance when she posed her question. He had learnt that when she looked at him in that way, it was usually because he had failed to consider something that was second nature to her but that she felt he ought to know just the same. After giving the matter some thought, Darcy spoke.

"I see your point." He then kissed her softly upon the cheek. "Let us return at any rate, so that I might pamper and spoil you excessively over the next few days, before we begin the arduous task of conceiving our first child."

"Arduous task! You make it sound so daunting."

"I imagine it very well may be. I intend to work very hard at this," he lovingly teased. "It shall be, in fact, my sole focus over the coming weeks."

"Certainly there will be other matters to address." She smiled up at him. "What about the estate?"

"What better way to manage the estate, as well as to secure its future, than to beget its heir?" Darcy asked. "It will be as though we are not even here, but rather we are off in town. I shall give the order that the master and mistress are in the process of creating the heir, and we are absolutely not to be disturbed for any reason at all."

Elizabeth laughed aloud at the prospect, especially as she envisioned how Mrs. Reynolds would communicate such a directive to Pemberley's staff.

~ ~ ~

Days turned into weeks as Darcy and Elizabeth once again fell back into some of their normal routines. Each day, weather permitting, they rose just after dawn and enjoyed brisk morning horseback rides about the estate. After breakfast and the completion of her household management duties, Elizabeth would eagerly set off on her solitary rambles, while Darcy was off in his study attending to estate matters. The grounds of Pemberley were her very own sanctuary. Elizabeth loved spending her time out of doors—with or without her husband's company. Her afternoons were shared with Darcy. The two never lacked for one form or another of entertainment—whether it was reading in the library or alfresco, in the many fields of Pemberley. Every evening began with informal dining with her husband and ended in the warm expanse of his arms.

Elizabeth often wrote to new friends she had made, as well as old. It seemed she exchanged letters with Georgiana on an almost daily basis. There was one letter, however, that Elizabeth sought more than anything else. At long last, she received it. It was a letter from Jane.

After finding a very comfortable resting place in one of her favourite alcoves, Elizabeth read the letter from her beloved sister once again.

Dearest Elizabeth,

Thank you for your letters. You must know how very much each and every one of them means to me. Though, you would not know any of that at all if you were to judge by my responses, or rather lack thereof. Let me assure you, after having spent as much time with you as I have this year, I find that I steadily miss you more and more each day.

Allow me to explain the reason for my neglect...

Jane went on to expound upon the many challenges she faced in bringing about a return to normalcy in the girls' routines, as well as that of her home. As Elizabeth read the letter, it was obvious that it was the product of many starts and stops. She spoke of so many things—of Longbourn, of Meryton, of Mrs. Bennet, as well as of Mary and Kitty. Somewhere along the line, the tone of the letter changed. Jane conveyed the news that could only bring joy to her sister's heart. She was with child.

As she had done initially, Elizabeth smiled with the reading of such a glad tiding. She clutched the letter tightly to her chest. Any lingering sense of unease that she may have harboured about her sister's chances for felicity, she completely brushed aside. Good things were happening—for everyone.

Of that, Elizabeth was thoroughly convinced.

~ ~ ~

It was the time of the year when it was much too warm to consider a fire, even at night. The Darcys decided to make do with a multitude of lighted candles arranged in the fireplace, thus fostering a decidedly romantic ambiance.

It was the night of their first wedding anniversary. Darcy and Elizabeth sat on the floor before the fireplace wrapped in one another's loving embrace, savouring their intimacy, when they heard a knock on the door. Darcy supposed it could only be his valet. He gave permission for him to enter. Mr. Walters walked in, bearing an enormous box, with a large, velvety bow on top. Darcy stood to retrieve the box and brought it over to his wife.

Elizabeth eagerly accepted his offering. She was quite startled once it was fully within her grasp. "Whatever can this be? There appears to be something moving inside!"

"Open it quickly and see for yourself what it is!"

Elizabeth opened the box and observed two big, adorable eyes staring up at her. "It is a puppy!" She was very excited as she reached into the box and handed the puppy out. She bestowed a warm, gentle cuddle. Darcy was down on his knees beside her, rubbing the puppy's soft coat. Elizabeth reached up to touch her husband's face before kissing his chin. "Thank you so much. This little fellow shall be an excellent companion for me, now that I have decided to forego our rides and resume my habit of long walks each morning."

"Forego our morning rides? I shall be very sorry about that!"

"I do not know. Perhaps you will be delighted when you discover my gift to you."

"Do you think so?" He leaned forward to kiss her lips. "Well, do not keep me in suspense. Where is it?"

"You will have to close your eyes." He did as she instructed. She placed his hand on her belly. "Open your eyes."

He did. Darcy's countenance varied from puzzlement, to enlightenment, to elation. "Are you telling me that I am to be a father?"

"Yes, my love!"

"You are quite certain?"

"Indeed, it is early yet, but all the signs suggest that it is true. There shall be an addition to our family in the spring. Are you pleased?"

"Indeed," he said, as he embraced her. He kissed her upon her temple, along the side of her face and lastly, upon her lips. "How shall we celebrate this wonderful occasion?"

"I leave that for you to decide."

"I can think of any number of variations, but in the end, there is only one thing I wish for," he murmured, as he positioned himself before her and began raising the hem of her gown."

"Do you ever think of anything else?"

"No—not ever," he whispered, in between kisses along her inner thigh.

"We are not alone or have you forgotten?"

"Of course we are...," continuing his efforts. "There is no one here but you and me."

Elizabeth looked over towards the new puppy. Darcy paused long enough to find out her meaning.

"Elizabeth, you cannot be serious."

"On the contrary—I am quite serious."

"Then, hold that thought." Darcy picked up the puppy, walked over to the door, and beckoned a footman over to attend to it. Closing the door, he quickly walked back to his wife to resume his abandoned position.

"Now—where were we?"

~ *Chapter 11* ~
To Be Suspect

Charles Bingley enjoyed the benefit of a standing invitation to visit his friend Darcy at Pemberley. That year, he took the opportunity to visit his old friend towards the end of summer.

Thus, the Darcys' idyllic sequester at Pemberley came to an abrupt end with the arrival of Bingley and Lady Grace, Mr. and Mrs. Hurst, and last, but not least, Caroline. Though Elizabeth was not apt to admit it, one of the reasons she had readily engaged the society of Lady Ellen and her circle, was to minimise the opportunities of socialising with Caroline whilst in town. The disadvantage to Elizabeth in that was she rarely saw Lady Grace, for the two were quite fond of one another.

Wandering, once again, about the great halls of Pemberley, Caroline just about forgot that she would never be mistress of the place. To that day, she wondered what did Eliza Bennet have that she did not possess, and when exactly did she lose her considerable power over Mr. Darcy. Caroline vacillated between, feigning deference to the so-called mistress and slipping back into her old pattern of thinly disguised condescension.

Having recalled her humiliation the last time she visited with the Darcys in town, she at least now knew better than to disparage Elizabeth outright. Rather, she went on and on reciting how Elizabeth had changed nothing at Pemberley and how remiss she was; for what else was there for her to do with her time?

"As much as I have always loved Pemberley, I have always anticipated any number of ways to improve upon it," Caroline remarked one afternoon, as the ladies were at tea. "Pray tell me Elizabeth, what alterations do you mean to make?"

"In truth, I have not given much thought to make any changes, as of yet."

"Of course, it is entirely likely that you have never seen many fine homes, and thus you have little to draw upon in the knowledge of contemporary decoration. I shall be happy to offer my counsel."

As they were now somehow on a first-name basis, Elizabeth replied, "I am sure you would, Caroline. I assure you that you need not bother. My husband and I are quite contented with the way things are."

At that moment, Darcy and Bingley walked into the room, the former carrying Elizabeth's puppy in his arms, cradled close to his chest. His intention was to hand it off to Elizabeth, but before he could, Caroline overtook him. Caroline had a strong affection for the breed—her own dog being of the same pedigree. She stood much too close to Darcy as she simpered and cooed over the small animal. When she extended her hand to pat its head, the puppy snapped at her, causing her to back off so abruptly she nearly tumbled over.

Neither Darcy nor Elizabeth had ever witnessed such an adverse reaction from the puppy towards anyone. Whilst Bingley moved swiftly to save his sister from falling, Darcy attempted to hush the puppy, for he had become quite agitated.

He whispered in the darling little puppy's ear, "Where have you been all my life?"

Rather than, take the little fellow to his wife, as he originally intended, Darcy decided to continue to hold the puppy himself while he visited with his guests. In fact, he would continue to be seen holding the puppy, whenever he was in the room with a certain annoying young woman. Darcy was amazed at just how powerful a repellent the puppy was against Caroline's tendency to attach herself to his person. He thought, *If only I had known.*

As they were rather late in the summer in embarking upon their journey to the north that year, the Bingley party did not stay at Pemberley beyond a week. As happy as Elizabeth was for the abbreviated stay, to have so little time with Lady Grace was the cause for regret. As was their custom, Elizabeth and Grace sought to spend as much time outside of the company of the Bingley sisters as good manners would afford.

Though Elizabeth did not share her joyous news with anyone besides her husband, including her dear friend Grace, thinking it was a little too early in her term; she was delighted to see, first hand, that Grace was of the same delicate constitution, only farther along. Grace shared with her that baby Bingley was expected by year's end. As overjoyed as Grace was in anticipation of the blessed occasion, she confided to Elizabeth, another matter for which she was equally ecstatic. Now that, Charles and she were about to start their own family, he had decided (though not without quite a bit of nudging by his wife) that it was time for his sister Caroline to have her own establishment; that or move in with the Hursts. Either choice did not matter to Lady Grace. The only thing that remained unsettled in the matter was the actual sharing of that fact with Caroline.

After the departing of one party of guests, the Darcys soon welcomed the arrival of another guest. On his way to his parent's country home, Richard decided to stop off at Pemberley first, as had been his custom for many, many years. His plan was to remain with the Darcys for under a week before journeying on to Matlock.

As to be expected, Darcy was pleased to see him, for it had been some months since they last saw each other. The two quickly fell into their familiar routine of daily riding, sporting, and the like—but now mindful of the need to spend the evenings with Elizabeth. Elizabeth could hardly complain. She spent more time than had been her habit napping each afternoon, with her little puppy curled beside her.

It seemed Richard had been fairly busy since he last saw his cousin. For one, he had resigned his commission in the military. The news came as a surprise to Darcy. Though, a pleasant surprise, for Darcy was glad to know that his cousin would no longer be potentially in harm's way. It was just that Richard had not mentioned his plans to do so beforehand, prompting Darcy to consider that it had not been a matter of long deliberation on his cousin's part.

The other matter of which Richard sought to apprise Darcy was not at all pleasant. It was certainly not something Darcy wished to discuss with his cousin ever again, for it regarded Antoinette—the courtesan who once resided at Madam Adele's establishment in town.

Richard had inadvertently discovered that she was married to a tenant farmer on a neighbouring estate of his parents' home in Matlock. He had seen her a while back in the local town with the man, made discreet inquiries, and found out how it all came to be.

Darcy asked, "What makes you think that I am interested in any of this?"

"One never knows about these things. There is always the spectre of temptation. In this case, it is looming just around the corner—literally."

"As a married man, I would certainly not be tempted. Even if, I were not married, by your own account, she undoubtedly is. Unlike you, Richard, I have never had nor will I ever suffer a proclivity for another man's wife."

"What makes you think that I ever have?"

"Perhaps you have not—keep it that way."

"Be that as it may, are you curious to know what else I have discovered about her?"

"Not really, but as you are no doubt anxious to tell me, I believe I am powerless to prevent you."

"Her name is actually…," Richard went on to reveal all that he had uncovered.

Darcy was astounded to know that she now lived in Derbyshire. Though, more annoyed by the message itself, rather than the messenger, he responded, "You should be glad then, that she was off-limits to you. You cannot miss that which you have never had."

"If you say so…," Richard retorted. The thought in the back of his mind being that his cousin seemed particularly upset to have learnt of this information. Richard considered though it was unlikely their paths should ever cross again, with the woman being so relatively close to the vicinity, it was better that Darcy be made aware of that fact—just in case.

Darcy thought he had heard the last of that chapter of his past, when his solicitor informed him over a year ago that the young woman had opted to leave her former life and had been re-established with a respectable family elsewhere in England. He did not venture to learn of the details. Never once did he imagine that of all the places in England, she had re-established her life somewhere in Derbyshire.

Interrupted from his pondering by the drone of his cousin's voice, Darcy brusquely cut him off. "Pardon me, Richard. I have some business that I must attend to at the moment. I shall see you at dinner."

Alone in his study, he was left to mull over the implication of Richard's words even further.

What Richard did not know, and therefore, was unable to share with Darcy, was that the young woman known to them as Antoinette had indeed lived with a respectable family for a spell, after leaving the brothel.

It was there that she caught the eye of her husband. He was a genial man of extremely modest means and the father of two young boys. Even with the knowledge of her past, he courted her properly, and soon afterwards, made her his wife. He brought his family back to his home in Derbyshire, where he hoped they would remain for the rest of their days; far from the life she had once known, far from anyone who might have knowledge of her past and perhaps judge her harshly.

⸙

Given the intimacy of their party, Darcy, Elizabeth, and Richard always dined in the small dining-room. They chose to remain together after dinner and venture straight away to the drawing-room where Elizabeth often times exhibited on the pianoforte. That evening, in particular, Richard sat next to Elizabeth to turn the pages, while Darcy stationed himself beside the instrument to enjoy the performance, whilst commanding a full view of his wife's lovely countenance.

Between songs, whilst scanning the music sheets to select another piece, Elizabeth remarked, "May I be one of the first to commend you on your service to our country, and express my well wishes for your success in your next endeavour. What do you suppose that might be?" When Darcy shared the news with her that Richard had resigned his commission, she fretted over what it might mean. *I certainly hope you do not mean to spend much of your time here at Pemberley.*

"That is very thoughtful of you to bestow your good wishes upon me. You need not fret. I am sure I will find a number of pleasant endeavours to undertake. Actually, it is I who should be wishing you joy, is it not?"

"You wish ME joy? Whatever for?" Elizabeth asked, thinking to herself how she might deal with her husband, for having confided such intimate details of their private life to Richard.

"Pardon me, madam. Did you intend that it should be kept a secret?"

Elizabeth's countenance spoke volumes. Darcy rubbed his finger along his cheek and then, shrugged his shoulders slightly. "I am sorry, Elizabeth. It is just that Richard has continued to express such a great concern for your welfare these past days."

With all the forbearance of civility, Elizabeth smiled. "I suppose that I shall simply have to make allowances for you two once again," Elizabeth said thinking it best to reproach her husband away from prying eyes. *As if it matters,* she considered. She wondered if there was anything that he did not share with his cousin. She continued, "I trust that I may rely upon your discretion to keep this to yourself. It should not be shared with the family just yet, *Cousin*." The slightly derisive emphasis on the appellation did not go unnoticed.

"You may depend upon my reputation as a gentleman, for my utmost discretion."

"And what of your reputation as an officer—pardon me, a former officer?" Elizabeth questioned half seriously, attempting to deflect her annoyance at the two men with a bit of levity. She had enough of her own thoughts of his reputation as a gentleman, to be suspect.

"Ah—yes! Rely upon my word as an officer and a gentle-man, my lady," Richard waxed poetically as he took her hand and raised it to his lips, prompting Darcy to roll his eyes at the exchange.

"Indeed, I shall depend upon it. Now, if you will excuse me, I find I have had quite enough entertainment for one evening." Elizabeth stood to leave the room. She stopped at the doorway and turned her attention towards the two men as they were about to have a drink.

"Join me, Mr. Darcy."

So much for an evening of entertainment with his cousin Richard…

~ *Chapter 12* ~
Live Vicariously

The Fitzwilliam family tradition was to receive a large party of guests at their country home each September. The Darcys had foregone the gathering the year before as they were on their honeymoon. Lady Ellen was overjoyed to receive them that year. Other guests included Lord Harry, Lady Georgiana, Lord and Lady Stafford, and Lady Harriette. Not to go unmentioned, Lady Catherine de Bourgh and her daughter Anne completed the guest list.

Lady Catherine typically eschewed the invitation. Lady Ellen and she had never really been on the best of terms, what with one endeavouring to play matchmaker between Darcy and an eligible lady of the *ton* and the other with her heart set upon a match with her daughter Anne. That year Lady Catherine eagerly accepted. Still aggrieved over the fact that Elizabeth had spurned the invitation to Rosings Park during Easter, Lady Catherine determined to avenge the perceived slight.

She did not intend to waste a single moment. The first night at dinner, she introduced the subject of the proud, aristocratic bearings of the Fitzwilliams and Middletons, and how exceedingly happy she was that young Georgiana had honoured her duty to the family in accepting the alliance. She spoke of Georgiana's marriage to Lord Harry as if it had been preordained by Lord Matlock and Lord Stafford, when the truth was that though the elder aristocrats greatly desired the match, they preferred to believe that it was the young people's own choice.

Lady Catherine cared not about the awkwardness of the conversation. She went into considerable detail in outlining the lineage of both families, engaging them all in conversation that they were apt to discuss, as it involved their own proud heritages. Even Lady Ellen and Lady Elise were drawn into the conversation to speak of their own lineages, both steeped in the aristocracy, as well.

Elizabeth was not feeling very well from the start and was not inclined to take part in the conversation. She felt very much an outsider. Thinking the discussion at hand was the sole source of Elizabeth's discomfort, Lady Catherine went on to discuss the distinctions in rank and privilege, and the inherent disadvantages of unequal alliances and marrying outside of one's own sphere. She spoke not a single word to Elizabeth during the entire discourse. The crafty old woman was extremely careful to speak in generalities, knowing as she did that should she come right out and say what was truly on her mind, that her brother would likely banish her from his home. She would not risk that. She had come to Matlock, specifically to wreak havoc on the Darcys' marriage.

When the ladies and gentlemen separated after dinner, the former adjourning to the drawing-room and the latter remaining seated for port and cigars, Lady Catherine stepped up her antics for a more direct assault upon Elizabeth. With neither Darcy nor her brother present, she thought she might seize the moment.

"Elizabeth, come sit next to me. I was not at all pleased that you declined the opportunity to visit Rosings Park this year. I should like to have a word with you."

"Certainly, Lady Catherine," Elizabeth said as she took the seat next to her.

"Pray tell, how is your family in Hertfordshire? Have you visited with them since your marriage to my nephew?"

"I have not had the occasion to visit them since they all joined us at Pemberley in December."

"Oh, yes of course, now that you mention it, I do recall my nephew bringing up that. All of your relatives are in trade in some form or fashion, is that not correct?"

"I dare not say all of them but yes, some of my relatives are in trade. It is no great secret."

Lady Catherine went on to speak disparagingly of her history with Mr. Collins and his role in the Bennet family's return to some level of respectability, to those closest to her in the room. When she eventually ensued upon a rapid series of questions to Elizabeth, designed to embarrass her of her family, Elizabeth determined that she had enough. She felt nauseated. She was sure it had nothing to do with her delicate condition. Her Ladyship caused her to be quite ill.

She arose from her seat. "Excuse me Lady Catherine, but I find that I have had all of your society that I can bear for one evening. Perhaps I will find you more tolerable in the morning. I bid you goodnight." Elizabeth turned her attention to everyone in the room. "Pardon me."

Lady Catherine was left with her mouth gaped wide open —such was her shock at being so summarily dismissed by the young upstart.

Georgiana was speaking intimately with her mother-in-law and sister-in-law through all of it. She missed the entire exchange. She did notice when Elizabeth quitted the room. Georgiana quickly took after her sister. "Elizabeth, are you quite all right? You look rather pale. What did my aunt say to you?"

"It is nothing of consequence. I am fine, just a little tired. I will see you in the morning." The two sisters embraced. Georgiana returned to the drawing-room, and Elizabeth went upstairs to her apartment.

Darcy only remained with the party long enough to learn from Georgiana that Elizabeth had left earlier. She shared her suspicions that their aunt had upset Elizabeth somehow.

He found Elizabeth standing in the dimly-lit room, staring into the mirror at her own reflection, with her arms wrapped about her. He approached her from behind and placed his hands on her waist. "Georgiana told me that Lady Catherine might have done something to upset you. I apologise for my aunt's callousness," he said between placing kisses along the length of her neck and shoulders.

"Is that your answer to everything?" Elizabeth asked her husband, drawing away slightly, after momentarily succumbing to his amorous designs.

In truth, he could not bear to be in the same room with her and not be touching her, especially when they were alone. He was drawn to her like a moth to a flame.

"I only wish to soothe you, and I believe you have found this very soothing at times." Darcy released his hands and stepped back. "If you prefer a hands-off approach, I am able to do that, as well. See," he teased as he raised his hands in the air. With his failed attempt at levity, he took her hand and led her to the couch to sit. "Please tell me what is truly troubling you."

"Why did you not stand up for me against your aunt?"

"What are you referring to?"

"I feel as though you completely abandoned me."

"I did no such thing. I was by your side during the entirety of dinner. It is customary for gentlemen to remain behind for a brief spell, before rejoining the ladies. I was only a short distance down the hall."

"You may as well have been in another town for all that you did to fend off your aunt's attack."

"I saw no reason to intervene. She was not attacking you personally. I admit she showed very poor taste in raising those particular subjects at all. But, what did she say that is not true? Would you have rather that I cause an even greater spectacle by insisting that she not discuss our family's heritage in your presence?"

"So, you agree with her then…, that it is degrading to marry someone so beneath you in consequence." Elizabeth was paraphrasing, for Lady Catherine had been particularly keen not to level so specific a charge, thus provoking everyone else's ire.

"Elizabeth, I agree that Lady Catherine exercised poor judgement in raising a subject that one might infer upon our own situation, but the views she expounded are widely held and not only in our circle but by society in general."

"Do I embarrass you? Are you ashamed of having married me?"

"Do not be ridiculous. Elizabeth, you know that I am not ashamed of you. I love you above everything else that I hold dear. I would be lost without you."

"I cannot help but look around us and see everyone here has roots in the aristocracy, everyone except me that is. If you had not married me, you too might have chosen a more suitable woman from your own sphere. Instead, you are forever bound to someone whose roots are entrenched in trade and servitude."

"If I had not married you, I would be a sad and forlorn old man, destined to wander the halls of Pemberley all alone for the rest of my days." Darcy pulled Elizabeth into his embrace. "I have never heard you speak this way. I can only surmise that it is a fleeting bout of melancholy, magnified by my callous aunt's prejudices. We are of the same sphere. You are my wife. You are to give birth to our child. You are just as entitled as anyone here."

Darcy kissed Elizabeth on her forehead. "Do not give my aunt another thought. You are no stranger to her. You know that if I chastise her on this matter it will only encourage her vitriol. Experience tells me, that she is not much capable of anything other than harsh words. Trust me when I say that I will not allow her or anyone to harm you."

Darcy meant every word of what he said. He meant to do all he could in protecting his wife from harm. Before they departed from Pemberley for the trip to Matlock and even with the unlikely chance that their paths should ever cross, he shared with Elizabeth, the information that Richard had confided of the woman from his past. He told her everything that Richard told him.

Elizabeth accepted the news as calmly as could be expected. At least, she had been informed she reckoned, and thereby prepared in the improbable occasion of a chance encounter.

~ ~ ~

Lady Catherine could not have been more pleased with herself; having witnessed Elizabeth quit the room the evening before. She decided to step-up the pressure even more; seeing how speaking a few well-timed truths had affected Elizabeth so. It seemed that destiny was on her side, for something that Lady Catherine had not counted upon had fortuitously presented itself to her. She could discern that the very beautiful and accomplished Lady Harriette Middleton appeared to fancy her nephew.

She decided to enlist the young lady in her scheme. It was very simple—to perpetuate a hoax designed to persuade Elizabeth that her husband was involved in an extra-marital indiscretion. Her Ladyship honestly thought Elizabeth was too naïve to understand the way things were in their sphere. She would not accept an unfaithful husband, even though it was generally accepted amongst the *ton*. In addition, the elderly woman was convinced that she would succeed in forcing Elizabeth to realise the enormous disadvantages she had brought upon her husband. After all, any young woman who sought to compare herself to the young Lady Harriette would surely find herself to be lacking, or so thought Lady Catherine.

The vindictive old woman was utterly convinced of the solidity of her plan. It was guaranteed to drive Elizabeth away from Darcy. Once she was forced to flee, then Darcy would be persuaded to divorce Elizabeth; freeing him up for Anne and the ultimate combining of the two great estates of Pemberley and Rosings Park. Astute enough to realise that Lady Harriette would have no inducement to go along with a scheme where she would end up empty-handed, Lady Catherine would endeavour to convince the young lady to go along by employing a bit of subterfuge. It was plain to see that she had designs on Darcy. Lady Catherine would persuade the young woman to believe that she would help foster and support an alliance with her soon to be divorced nephew.

Lady Harriette could be as calculating as could Lady Catherine. She feigned deference to the elderly woman without venturing to express her own thoughts on the matter. Having heard her piece, she could hardly wait to flee her presence. *Does her Ladyship believe I was born yesterday? Everyone in the ton knows of her ambition to have Fitzwilliam married to her own daughter. She must think I am a complete idiot. I will show her!*

Lady Catherine could see that Lady Harriette had not dismissed her words out of hand. In fact, the young woman seemed to give the matter careful consideration. She determined to press on.

"What say you, young lady? Time is of the essence. Who is to say when an opportunity, such as we now have before us, will present itself once more?"

"I will think on the matter, Your Ladyship. That is the best that I can offer at present." Lady Harriette moved to escape the elderly woman as fast as she could. *I am determined that I shall have Fitzwilliam, and I need no help from you—you delusional old woman! Thank you very much!*

~ ~ ~

Lord Matlock was beside himself that morning, just having received an account from one of his associates, of his son Richard's conduct in town. True, Richard was a grown man of nearly three and thirty. However, having retired his commission, the bulk of his current income was fully at the discretion of his father.

He barged into the billiard-room and demanded a word with his son. Not at all surprised in finding him there with Darcy, Lord Matlock insisted that his nephew stay where he was. It was time that both men heard what he was about to say.

He glanced from his son to Darcy, then back to his son with sheer exasperation. Eventually, he asked, "What is this that I hear of you carousing about town, behaving and thinking as if you are still a young man?"

Richard was taken aback slightly by his father's stern mien. It was certainly not the first time that someone had thought to tell his father of such matters.

"What is it that has you so concerned this time?" Richard asked nonchalantly, whilst thinking to himself, *the sooner you get this over with, the sooner I can take this next shot.*

Lord Matlock looked at his son with dismay. For an instant, he was convinced that there stood before him, one of the two most self-absorbed men he had ever known—the other stood a few feet off to his side.

"Where do I begin?" Lord Matlock tossed over the letter he received from his acquaintance in town, outlining Richard's exploits, upon the billiard-table. Richard picked it up promptly, for his own inspection.

Lord Matlock was extremely disappointed. "Why on earth do you continue to behave much the same as you did in the days of your youth? You are always engaged in frivolous pursuits!"

Directing his gaze to his nephew, he continued. "And you, Darcy, despite having taken the step of marriage—you are as inclined as ever to live vicariously through Richard, as if nothing has changed!"

The older man returned his attention to Richard. "I will no longer abide such recklessness, I tell you. I will say this only once, son. You WILL settle down and marry, even if I have to select a bride for you myself, or I will cut you off financially. Darcy here may be willing to finance your debauchery indefinitely, but I certainly will not. It is beyond time for you to grow up...BOTH of you!"

Lord Matlock did not stay to entertain questions. He stormed out of the billiard-room in a huff.

Once the two men were alone, Richard opined to his cousin of the injustice of it all; to be spied upon and scrutinised constantly. To his astonishment, Darcy would have none of it. He agreed with his uncle.

"Your father is right, you know. We have been wrong to keep holding on to our youth; refusing to let go as if our behaviour of the past constitutes appropriate behaviour today. Our yesterdays have long gone by.

"Far be it from me to tell you how to live your life, but I too believe it is time to put childish things aside. It is time we move forward. I am guilty in all of this in my complacency, but surely, you see that this cannot go on.

"I too must stop fostering you, while you waste away your life."

"Or perhaps, you simply wish to appease your wife." Richard lashed out at Darcy in an irate tone.

"Elizabeth knows nothing of this. I assure you. I imagine if she did, it would infuriate her. As it is, she is driven to distraction by our close bond. This is not about her. It is about us. I wish to see you pursue a different path…, one that leads to fulfilment and joy in the comfort of knowing that you have someone with whom to share your life."

"You mean to say that you wish to see me as miserable as you have been of late!" Richard retorted.

"Do not disparage it, unless you have tried it, my friend. Surely, there is a woman for you somewhere who might assist you in that endeavour."

Richard resigned himself rather quickly to the inevitable—even he realised a change was long overdue. His mood lightened. He thought about what Darcy said. After a moment, he continued. "Only one woman comes to mind. You know her quite well."

"Elizabeth's sister," Darcy alleged. "Surely you jest!"

"Actually, it is your sister's dear sister, Lady Harriette, of whom I speak. She is the embodiment of everything I would wish for in a wife."

"I imagine that her dowry of 50,000 pounds only adds to the appeal. Which reminds me," Darcy said, as he took the missive, that had just been handed to him that morning, from his pocket, and passed it to Richard.

The note bore Lady Harriette's seal. It was elegantly inscribed *Fitzwilliam*.

"It is a note from the very captivating young lady herself…, addressed to Fitzwilliam. Why do you pass it to me unread? It is most likely intended for you."

"It is hardly appropriate for a young maiden to address a note to a married man," Darcy remarked.

"Indeed," Richard pocketed the note for his later perusal. "Nothing ventured. Nothing gained."

Lady Harriette had been very encouraged by the fact that when she placed the note in Darcy's own hand, he did not object in the least bit. Rather, he eyed the note curiously and then placed it in his pocket; leaving no doubt in her mind that he would read it at leisure and comply with her wishes.

When Lady Harriette passed the note to Darcy, she was unaware that the entire exchange had been observed.

~ ~ ~

Amidst the still of the night, he entered the room without even a light tap at the door. He espied her as she rested on her bed, with her long tresses flowing across the bed covers, and with an opened book at her side. She had obviously fallen asleep whilst awaiting the arrival of her clandestine visitor. He had seen many beautiful women thus; none compared to the vision before him.

He approached her bedside, and admired her a few moments longer before leaning forward and placing his hand gently upon her shoulder.

"Lady Harriette."

She stirred. The pleasant smile on her face quickly faded as she realised it was not the *Fitzwilliam* she had invited to her apartment. She sat up immediately.

"Colonel Fitzwilliam! What on earth are you doing in my room?"

He showed her the note, "Am I not invited?"

"You know very well that I intended that note for your cousin! How did it come into your possession?"

"He handed it to me. He IS married, you know. Why would he assume that you intended the note for him?"

"This is not to be borne. Leave my room immediately or I shall…, I shall scream!" threatened she.

"That would be unfortunate, seeing as I have a written invitation to be here. But, do not worry; I shall not divulge your little scheme."

"What is it that you want of me?"

"I am here to put an end to your trifling affection for Darcy. You, young lady, have been playing a dangerous game. I mean for you to stop."

She was about to protest further. He silenced her by placing his finger upon her lips.

"Can you even imagine the damage that might have been caused had this note fallen into the wrong hands?

"You are an incredibly beautiful young woman. Why would you even consider throwing yourself away for something that will never be? Even if you could persuade him to join you in your bed, which I daresay; there is little to no possibility of, you can never hope to have more than a fleeting romance at best. He will never leave his wife. She means everything to him."

"She does not deserve him! She is not his equal, and I do not believe she loves him!"

"That is not for you to say. His heart belongs to her. Do you imagine yourself to be in love with him or is it simply the challenge of wanting something you can never have…, you having never been denied anything before?"

She gave no answer.

At that moment, they heard the sounds of someone attempting to gain entry into the room. Very astutely, Richard remembered to lock the door when he entered, thereby thwarting the intentions of the outsider. The unmistakable sound of receding footsteps signalled the person's departure down the hall.

Still sitting on the bed beside her, Richard continued. "You and I are so much alike, my dear Harriette. You are passionate, adventurous, and defiant. You are my equal in every way, and everything I would wish for in a lover.

"I am hereby putting you on notice," he said, as he leaned closer towards her. "I intend to court you," he whispered softly in her ear, sending pleasurable sensations of fright along her spine. "To win your heart," he murmured, as he gently trailed his fingertips along the décolletage of her nightgown, drew tiny circles about her taunt nipples, and halted his path near the centre of her bosom. "To marry you," he pledged as he kissed her lips, tenderly at first, slowly increasing the smooth pressure, second by second, till only her soft moans were able to recall him to the surroundings.

Moments later, he was gone.

Within minutes, Lady Catherine returned with a footman, to open the door. She had been the one to see Lady Harriette hand the note to Darcy. The elderly lady feared she had been duped. Their scheme did not call for any such alteration! She was determined to defeat the young lady at her own game. Entering the room, she saw Lady Harriette sitting up in her bed, alone, and looking quite contented.

"What on God's earth just happened here? Where is my nephew?"

~ *Chapter 13* ~
No Cause to Repine

L ady Harriette woke that morning with her mind full of a certain Fitzwilliam. Court *her*. Win *her* heart. Marry *her*. When in her life had she been issued such a blatant challenge?

It was not as though it was her first kiss. She remembered her first kiss ever with a young man a few years back. She certainly had never been kissed as she had been the night before. Heretofore never experienced feelings tingled deep inside of her as she recalled his lips upon hers. She was simply unable to suppress a girlish smile. *Court her. Win her heart. Marry her.* When in her life had she been offered such a promising prospect?

Lady Ellen knew at the start that she would have to keep her sister in her sights as best she could. Knowing that Catherine was not keen on Darcy's marriage, she would have been surprised if her sister had not accepted the invitation to Matlock, purposely to cause trouble.

That little subterfuge at dinner had hardly gone unnoticed. However, seeing how her wily sister had not crossed any lines, speaking affectionately of her own proud heritage and encouraging everyone else to do the same, Lady Ellen felt that there was no cause to draw any more attention than was warranted to Elizabeth's possible discomfort.

The untimely speech about unequal alliances pushed the boundaries somewhat. There again, Lady Ellen believed that Elizabeth would bear it with grace and poise, after witnessing her hold her own amongst the elites of the *ton* so many times before. She was quite proud of Elizabeth in that.

She missed the later exchange in the drawing-room, however. It was only the way Elizabeth quitted the room that drew her attention.

Familiar with Elizabeth's habits, Lady Ellen altered her own morning routine to accompany her on her walk. When Elizabeth shared the news that she was expecting a child, Lady Ellen embraced her with tears in her eyes. This was indeed the news that she had longed to hear.

Her Ladyship was elated and at the same time concerned. The last thing her niece needed was uncalled-for stress. She endeavoured to get Elizabeth to share what had happened that first night, but Elizabeth was not forthcoming. She ventured to guess that which Elizabeth did not readily confess.

"You need not make a secret of it, my dear. I know my sister. I know how thoughtless and spiteful she can be when she feels she has been aggrieved.

"Your marriage to Fitzwilliam shattered her dreams. She is bound and determined to interfere in your marriage and make your life as miserable as her own."

"Yes—I believe you in that. Her Ladyship has made it quite clear that she does not approve of me."

"You need not be bothered by her. You are as dear to me as is Georgiana and Elise. I will not stand idly by and allow her to cause trouble for you and my nephew, especially now that there is your unborn child to consider."

"I find I am perfectly capable of standing up to her Lady-ship. I appreciate your kind words and support, even so."

Given the number of times the two headstrong women had butted heads over the past year, Lady Ellen had no doubts there. Speaking from experience, she replied, "I am quite certain of your ability to speak your own mind, my dear. Just know that you are not alone in this.

"Your dear husband, bless his heart, has managed far too long paying no heed to Lady Catherine's rudeness to understand how hurtful her words can be. Is it any wonder that he allowed her to go on thinking that he might marry Anne, for so many years, when he might have easily silenced her with a few well-chosen words?

"I, however, know exactly what my sister is capable of. I have a long history of dealing with her. I will keep a closer eye on her from this moment on. Should I see any sign of trouble, I shall invite her to hasten her departure from my home."

"I would hope it does not come to that. I have learnt to dislike her Ladyship, but I have grown very fond of Anne. I would hate to see her suffer a break from the family because of me."

Lady Ellen squeezed Elizabeth's hand. "You are very thoughtful to consider Anne's feelings. You are correct—she is the one who would suffer most, should it ever come to that. Let me think about that for a bit. In the meantime, you are not to trouble yourself at all over Lady Catherine. I will see to it personally that she stays in line for the remainder of her stay."

"Thank you, Lady Ellen."

"It is my pleasure dear."

And so, she did. As time went by, Lady Ellen used every trick in the book to keep Lady Catherine out of Elizabeth's path, even if it meant considerable discomfort to herself in having to engage her sister's company so regularly. Her scheme seemed to pay off. Lady Catherine appeared to grow less and less bothered by Elizabeth and for some odd reason, which Lady Ellen could not make out, more and more perturbed by Lady Harriette.

~ ~ ~

If anyone had told Colonel Richard Fitzwilliam that things would turn out as they had, he would have laughed. Young Lady Harriette Middleton was formidable; not like the ladies he usually sweet-talked and cajoled. He vowed to win the heart of the beautiful heiress and to marry her. How could he have known just what he was embarking upon?

It was as if he had completely forgotten; this young lady did not play by the rules. She made her own rules and what rules they were. It appeared that Lady Harriette had turned the tables on Richard. He thought to be the aggressor and the one to control the *courtship*, but she had other ideas.

Lady Harriette had always exercised her free will to spend time with Richard and Darcy, when she chose. It had almost reached the point that whenever the two gentlemen were to-gether, so there was she—the most notable exception being after dinner, when the men customarily separated from the wo-men.

Darcy, Richard, and Lady Harriette were on their way back to the stables after a strenuous morning ride. Lady Harriette had longed abandoned side-saddled riding and found she was able to keep up with them, for the most part. Neither was inclined to ignore her when she joined them on their outings. Both were willing to make allowances for her. When the situation called for it, she was not above resorting to her feminine wiles to gain the upper hand on the two cousins.

Just when Darcy had begun to accustom himself to their uncanny threesome, and somewhat relax in Lady Harriette's presence; Richard was beginning to feel the danger of her continued company. Riding up ahead of Darcy, he felt that he would have a few words with the young lady.

Richard rode along beside her for a few minutes in silence —racking his brain in search of the right words to say, when Lady Harriette stole his thunder.

"Colonel Fitzwilliam, I am of a mind to spend part of the morning exploring the outskirts of the estate. I require a gentleman escort. Are you quite up to the task?"

Richard had not planned to have his day arranged for him. He intended to spend the day as he had done the day before, sporting around the estate with his cousin and trying to elude her. While he had every intention of wooing the young lady, he would much rather it to be on his own terms.

"Lady Harriette, I am increasingly concerned over the nature of our acquaintance. As a young maiden, I feel you are not properly guarding your reputation. It is unseemly that you should wish to spend so much time in the exclusive company of two gentlemen."

"But sir, it is *you* with whom I wish to spend my time. Is it my fault that you seem never to part with your cousin?"

"There is a time for a gentleman to be seen keeping company with a young lady, and there is a time for a gentleman to keep company with like-minded gentlemen."

"I am not familiar with that rule. Is it one of yours?"

"Indeed it is not. It is a matter of convention."

"Ah—convention! Would this be the same convention by which you initiated our courtship?"

Richard coloured. He recovered. "Perhaps, from this moment forward, a more formal approach is warranted. You are no longer welcome to join me on outings such as this, and I will at-

tempt to refrain from interrupting *you* during your daily feminine pursuits."

"Feminine pursuits, indeed! When have you known me to
spend my time thus?"

"That is exactly my point. I suggest you spend more time
doing just that, and less time racing about on horseback, fencing, in billiard-rooms, and the like."

"Is there anything else that you wish to change about my
behaviour, sir?"

"Let us start with the few things I have suggested."

"As you wish, sir," Lady Harriette responded meekly.

They rode along in silence. Richard was quite pleased with
himself, as his countenance attested. *Who knew that all that was
required was a stern speech? That was far easier than I had
imagined. Darcy could learn a thing or two on how to handle
his woman from me.*

~ ~ ~

Richard and Darcy were in the billiard-room, the next day, when
a footman entered bearing a note in the familiar feminine script
that read, *Colonel Fitzwilliam*. Richard reluctantly accepted and
perused the note before putting it in his pocket.

The look upon his face prompted Darcy to ask tauntingly,
"Another command performance from your dear *betrothed*?"
How could he resist? It was her second summons of the day.
Earlier, she had sent Richard a note requesting that he join her
for a mid-morning stroll.

"Lady Harriette wishes for my presence in the east drawing-room."

"Then, by all means—make haste. You would not wish to
have her come after you," Darcy jested.

"I have no intention of responding to her summons. I will see her in my own time."

The game continued, but only to be interrupted twenty minutes later by the same footman, bearing yet another note. It flatly read, *"Now!"*

The gentlemen halted the game, donned their jackets and proceeded with alacrity to join Lady Harriette in the drawing-room. With a temperament like hers, neither of the two men was quite certain what she might be capable of—neither wished to find out. They found her with Elizabeth, Georgiana, Elise, and Anne. They were sitting about the room busily engaged in needlepoint and knitting with baskets of yarn and threads of pastel colours all about. Darcy went to Elizabeth's side to take a seat and examine her work.

"What is this that you are working on, my love?" Darcy fingered the tiny object in wonderment.

"It is to be one in a pair of stockings for our little Darcy. Can you not tell?" Elizabeth feigned astonishment that he could not make it out for himself.

"Oh—yes, yes of course," he quickly assented, as he continued to finger the tiny knitted object in bemusement.

It seemed that the excitement of more than one expected birth was shared widely. Georgiana was eager to share the news of her own pregnancy with Elizabeth almost as soon as they arrived in Matlock; Elizabeth confided her secret, as well. That particular morning they shared the news with the rest of the ladies at breakfast. Thus, the day was to be spent hand-knitting little infant articles. Though knitting was not the most fashionable pastime for aristocratic ladies at the time, Elizabeth and Georgiana thought it might be fun. They easily persuaded the others to try their hand at it, as well.

Having been banished from the gentlemen's company, and her own brother's company, as well, Lady Harriette was beside herself with the notion of being engaged in such an uninteresting pastime. She determined to have some fun at the Colonel's expense.

Richard approached the young woman. "Lady Harriette, you beckoned?"

"Oh yes! We have been discussing a matter that I feel requires a gentleman's opinion. As you know, there is not another gentleman on earth whose opinion I value more highly than yours, sir." She gestured for him to take a seat beside her on the settee.

"Sir, would you be as kind as to lend me your hands?"

"My hands? You seek my opinion, do you not?"

"As it turns out, I require both your hands *and* your opinion." She immediately started wrapping her knitting yarns about his extended hands.

Richard was growing more and more annoyed by the second. *Does she honestly expect me to go along with this?*

"Lady Harriette!"

"Thank you kindly for offering me your services, sir. I think my work here will flow much more smoothly now that I have you beside me to keep the yarns from becoming one tangled mess. Whatever would I do without you?"

"I have no time for this," he whispered, "What do you wish to ask?"

"Colonel Fitzwilliam, the ladies and I are engaged in a heated debate. We require your opinion to help us settle the matter." She attracted everyone's attention with that pronouncement. "We are simply unable to reach a consensus. Some say that the colour of this yarn is closest to that of the sky when the sun is at its highest. Others say the colour most closely matches that of the sky just hours before the sun sets. What say you?"

Richard looked at her as if she were mad. *What have I gotten myself into?*

Darcy found the entire exchange hard to ignore. He smirked at Richard when Lady Harriette was not looking (neither of them was quite willing to cross her at that point, feeling she was not the most predictable young woman they ever met).

"Surely, you must have an opinion on this matter," Darcy goaded his cousin, "what with your illustrious military background and all."

Richard most certainly did not have an opinion. He was at a complete loss for words.

"Take your time to decide, Colonel Fitzwilliam," Lady Harriette replied. "After all, we ladies do so enjoy these delightful feminine pursuits. We are quite at leisure."

~ ~ ~

Georgiana was anxious to question her sister Harriette regarding her unconventional relationship with her cousin. She thought she knew her sister very well. She was not apt to stand by uncaring whilst Harriette played her games.

"What on earth is going on between Cousin Richard and you? He is a good man. I would hate to think you are simply trifling with him for reasons known only to yourself." *Perhaps in another lame attempt to attract my brother's notice, supposing him to be jealous.*

"Georgiana, you are quite severe on me. You would likely not think so highly of your dear cousin if you really knew what he was about."

"What have you to accuse him of?"

"Oh, nothing really. The fact of the matter is that your cousin and I are engaged in a courtship of a peculiar sort. I simply intend to torment him a while longer for the manner of his *proposal*," Lady Harriette said, all the while thinking that if Georgiana had no knowledge of her cousin's reputation, she certainly would not be the one to enlighten her.

She continued, "With respect to *said* proposal, I feel your good opinion might be considerably altered, if you knew the truth of the matter."

"I am not afraid to risk it. I am sure whatever it was, it could not have been as inappropriate as you insinuate; otherwise, you would not have consented. Pray tell me how it came to be."

"I think not, dear sister. A lady must have her secrets." At that moment, she leisurely strolled over to her window. She had been keeping an eye out for Richard. At last he had returned, along with Darcy and her brother. The gentlemen had enjoyed a morning of shooting—yet another favourite pastime of hers from which she was now strictly forbidden by none other than Richard. She had concocted plans for him to make up for his latest directive. Lady Harriette returned her attention to Georgiana. "If you will pardon me, dear sister, I see that your cousin has just returned."

Georgiana decided to let the matter rest; convinced as she was, that Harriette's schemes did not centre on her brother. Still, she could not help but wonder what her husband might think to hear his young maidenly sister speak so.

As extended guests at Matlock, Darcy and Elizabeth were not at leisure to slip away, just the two of them, as often as they would have liked. With so many relatives about, there was always someone in want of either or both of their attention.

The two cherished their night-times. Darcy's favourite pastime of making love to his wife had not abated. Basking in the moments after a passionate interlude, he lay on his back and studied her face as she partially sat up, her head resting on her hand. He traced the back of his fingers along her bare shoulders as she spoke.

"I do not suppose there will be many nights like this in the months to come."

"Why ever not?"

"Look at me," she stated, pointing out her slight bulge.

Darcy traced her cheeks. "You are more beautiful than ever."

Elizabeth leaned forward and kissed his lips. "Only you would imagine such a thing."

"I am not imagining it. You are exquisite. Trust me when I say that we will always have nights like this. I will have to be gentler, is all." Darcy continued to caress her cheek, his eyes tracing a path from her eyes to her lips, whenever she spoke.

"And creative," she teased.

Darcy laughed. "Yes—very creative." His lips captured hers. "I assure you I have already begun to imagine just how creative I shall be. I can hardly wait."

Elizabeth moved closer as he opened his arm to encircle her in his embrace.

"There is a matter that I have meant to discuss with you."

"What is it, my love?"

"What do you think of Lady Harriette these days?"

"I do not think of her," he quickly asserted.

"Pardon me if I do not take you at your word on that."

Darcy ceased his tender caress to place his hand on his bare chest. "Why would you doubt me?"

"She is incredibly beautiful. She spends far more time than she ought with Richard and you, and anyone who has ever observed her closely in your presence during the past two years, can see that she has been overly infatuated with you."

"Interesting," Darcy said, as he contemplated Elizabeth's words. He wondered why Elizabeth had never shared her observations of Lady Harriette's unguarded behaviour before, and why on earth she thought to bring it up at that moment.

"Is it my imagination or has Harriette transferred her affections from you to your cousin?"

"I am not sure how to answer that question."

"I am rather sure you do."

"I mean to say, I do not know how she feels about Richard. I know that he admires her and is set upon winning her heart."

Elizabeth reflected on his words for a moment. She smiled at this new revelation. *Well, well, well. If he is unable to discern that Lady Harriette is interested in Richard, perhaps he indeed had no indication that she had been so affected by him for so long. Men!*

Elizabeth continued, "So, it does not bother you at all that the young woman who once had her heart set upon capturing you, is now intent on capturing your best friend."

"Do you really suppose that Lady Harriette fancies Richard?"

"Yes, I do. She delights in toying with him, mind you, and stringing him along, but I think she is quite taken. So how do you feel about that?"

"If she is indeed as enamoured of Richard as you seem to think, I hope that they will soon find their way to one another and that they will be very happy together. Does that satisfy?"

"Quite; to see your cousin Richard, settled—married to a woman such as Lady Harriette. I could not be more pleased than I am." Elizabeth confessed, "I cannot imagine a more worthy companion—for either of them than each other."

"Pray tell me, you do not harbour resentment towards Richard for his friendship with Jane."

"Why would you say such a thing? Did I not express my great pleasure of the match?"

"Yes—but it is the way you express your pleasure that gives me pause."

Thinking to herself how Lady Harriette manages to lead Richard around by the nose, Elizabeth said, "Let me assure you, sir, I only have your cousin's best interests at heart."

~ ~ ~

The picturesque spot that Richard picked for their outing afforded a magnificent view of the Matlock estate just off to the west. With a host of servants at their disposal to arrange the very elegant outdoor picnic and attend to their every need, the younger adults were all settled upon blankets, fully anticipating an afternoon of leisure. All the elderly relatives remained at the manor, thinking such an adventure as an afternoon spent out-of-doors on such a hot day was fool-hearty. Although, if any of them would but admit it, it was likely just the sort of thing they would have appreciated during a prior decade or two.

The familial setting made for a decidedly casual and relaxed atmosphere. All the gentlemen discarded their jackets in surrender to the sun's warmth. After partaking of the feast of cold meats, fruit, cakes and wine, some of the party decided to wander about the countryside. Georgiana and her husband set off in one direction, while Lady Harriette and Richard set upon another. Darcy and Elizabeth remained behind with Lord Robert, Lady Elise and Anne. The latter three conversed amongst themselves, while Darcy relaxed on his back with his head in Elizabeth's lap as she read her book.

Richard had yet to declare himself formally to Lady Harriette, but to anyone who would observe them closely, there was clearly an understanding of some sort between them.

"You look well today, Lady Harriette," Richard said.

"You are welcome to look," Lady Harriette retorted. With her arm linked with his, she teasingly closed any visible gap between them and eagerly continued, "Oh, when shall we announce our engagement, my dear dearest *Fitzwilliam*, for I am beside myself with joy?" She stressed the name Fitzwilliam, longingly and with deep affection, as she so often did when in Richard's sole company. She delighted in vexing him. Nothing vexed him more than that.

"Announce our engagement, Lady Harriette! Why! I have not even proposed to you as of yet."

"Then, is it not time that you do? I cannot account for this delay on your part. Mind you, I expect a proper proposal, with you on your knees and all that entails."

"A gentleman likes to think that he is in command of these matters. And another thing, I have not consented to be called by my surname. It is the most ridiculous notion I have ever heard."

"It is no more ridiculous than for you to declare your intention to me, for the sole purpose of controlling my fortune of 50,000 pounds. That I should be allowed to address you thus, is a trivial matter in comparison."

"You are quite mistaken, madam. My conduct in your apartment was unpardonable. I am obliged to marry you after having compromised you so thoroughly. However, if you continue to insinuate that it is indeed my cousin whom you desire…, well, I shall be forced to renege."

"To me, you two are cut from the same cloth. I would just as soon have one as the other; he, being the one, and you, being the other. Seeing that I cannot possibly have the one, as you so graciously pointed out, in my apartment no less, the other will do quite nicely. As long as you give me leave to address you as *Fitzwilliam*, I shall have no cause to repine."

"I shall not be satisfied to think you are simply transferring your affections from the one to the other. For Heaven's sake, I shall not be a surrogate for my cousin."

"I have always admired you, sir. I have never been indifferent to your many amiable qualities; far from it. Whereas, it has always been my intention to make a match with a gentleman whose fortune is suitable to my own, you have quite upset my plans."

"Lady Harriette, are you saying then that you truly desire me and not my cousin?"

"Come now, *Fitzwilliam*, do you truly believe that I would affirm feelings for you which I have no certainty of being reciprocated?"

"If you are waiting for me to be the first in this relationship to affirm said feelings, you are in for a long wait. Heavens help the man who truly falls in love with you," Richard said, all the while knowing just how deeply his heart was engaged already.

"We shall see about that."

~ *Chapter 14* ~
Reluctant Suitor

After all the taunting that Darcy had suffered from his cousin with respect to his relationship with Elizabeth, he was taking a great deal of pleasure in teasing Richard over his strange courtship with Lady Harriette. Acting as if an older brother of sorts, he pressed Richard on his intentions towards the young woman. In a lighter note, he wanted to know what Richard planned to do to prove himself worthy of Lady Harriette's hand.

Along those lines, Darcy asked, "What on earth are you waiting for to ask Lord Stafford's permission to court his daughter properly?"

Richard declared, "Why would I rush into anything formal, when it is such fun wooing Lady Harriette?"

"It certainly looks like it," Darcy attested sarcastically, while trying his best to refrain from laughter. Preparing for his next billiards shot, he asked, "How shall you like matrimony, you, who are so easily bored?"

"I daresay that I shall like it just as much as you, my friend."

"Indeed…, then, you shall be a very happy fellow, for I could not be more satisfied with my situation."

"Ah yes…, that I imagine you are; to have to look upon one woman, the same woman from now until the end of your days. What joy!"

"God willing that it should always be so. That you too shall have the privilege of looking upon one woman, the same woman henceforth, I have no doubts, my friend. I cannot imagine Lady Harriette as one to share anything. You had better accustom yourself to it."

~ ~ ~

Only days before all the guests were set to leave Matlock in return to their own homes, Darcy and Elizabeth were out for a ride in one of Lady Ellen's carriages when they spotted what looked to be Richard, just up ahead. He was not alone. He was with Lady Harriette. He appeared to be before her on a bent knee. Not wishing to interrupt what was obviously an intensely private moment, Darcy drew the vehicle to a halt.

"Whatever shall we do? It would be uncouth to interrupt such an intimate moment, but to stay here is equally untenable," Elizabeth said.

"Perhaps I should manoeuvre this around, and we can simply head back."

On their way back to the manor house, both could not help but laugh at the irony of the spectacle they had just seen.

"What do you find so amusing?" Darcy asked, even as he attempted to rein in his own laughter.

"I do not know…, it is just that I never considered that Lady Harriette would make your cousin work so hard to earn that which she was so eager to bestow all along."

"I hope he will be very happy. I am quite certain he deserves a bit of happiness."

"If you say so," said she. With an inkling of cynicism, she continued, "Perhaps he shall be the happiest man in all of England."

"Impossible, it is far more likely he shall be the second happiest, for I am the happiest man in all of England; the happiest and the luckiest because I have the great fortune of sharing my life with you."

~ ~ ~

"Why should I marry you? Give me one good reason," Lady Harriette beseeched her, hitherto, reluctant suitor.

Richard was flabbergasted. *Has she not pressured me for days to state my intentions, on bent knees, no less?*

Richard had barely slept a wink the past evening. He knew there was no point in putting the inevitable off any longer. Besides, he wanted to do so before everybody left Matlock in return to their own homes. Though, to his way of thinking, there could be no doubt of the outcome, he was quite nervous, even so. There he was, his moment of truth, poised to take the biggest step of the rest of his life. She stood there with her arms folded. Her lovely face bore the sternest expression he had yet to behold. She seemed not at all inclined to make it easy for him.

He raised himself to a standing position. "A reason?"

"Yes," she insisted, "I would bring 50,000 pounds to the alliance. What precisely are you offering?"

"Why—why my undying love for you!"

"You love me?"

"Yes, I do Harriette. I am very much in love with you. Indeed, my greatest wish is that you might one day return my love."

"Oh *Fitzwilliam*," she started. He gently touched his finger upon her lips to shush her. She was rendered silently attentive by the exquisite feelings thus provoked.

"Stop that."

"Richard, I do apologise for teasing you so," she said as she kissed him lightly upon his cheek. "If you must know, I absolutely adore you."

Richard and Lady Harriette soon returned to the manor house from their walk. He quietly spoke to Lord Harry to inquire of Lord Stafford's whereabouts. Told that he might be found in the library, Richard ventured there straight away. He was relieved to find him alone. Lady Harriette had forewarned him not to expect an eager audience in her father. Richard should not have been at all surprised as he found himself standing before the proud man, pleading his case.

"I am thinking of withholding my consent," declared he. "What say you to that?"

"Begging your pardon, my Lord," said Richard, "I find that unlikely, what with the close connections between our two families."

"Yes, your mother is Lady Stafford's dearest friend. Your father is one of my own closest friends." With his spectacles perched near the end of his bulbous nose, Lord Stafford drew a long whiff from his pipe. "Do not think those ties hold any sway over me, one bit. He has told me all about your debauchery over these past years. He would understand my decision that I might wish for a better man for my daughter. I assure you our relationship would suffer no damage at all."

Richard soon came to know that his verbal skirmishes with Lady Harriette were trivial in comparison to the interview with her father. Indeed, he found himself effectively having to sing for his suffer for the next half hour or so. It felt an eternity. At length, he was dismissed from Lord Stafford's company with a summons to send in Lady Harriette.

Relieved to be on his way, Richard opened the door of the library to see Lady Harriette standing there. "Your father wishes to see you," were his only words, accompanied by a puzzled look and a hint of a smile.

Her own anxiety could scarcely be contained as she had stood outside the library for the past quarter of an hour. She walked through the door left opened by her bewildered betrothed. Her father was walking about the room, looking grave and anxious. Immediately, upon espying his daughter, his aggrieved countenance gave way to a caring smile, as it always did, whenever he regarded her. Reared in the image of his deceased sister, his twin sibling who passed away during the year of her sixteenth birthday, young Harriette was christened with her late aunt's name. Lord Stafford certainly knew that moment would one day come; he never supposed that his daughter might lose her heart to a scoundrel! The words of his favourite playwright were brought to mind as he studied her intently. *She's beautiful, and therefore, to be woo'd. She is woman, therefore, to be won.*

"Harriette, my dear," said he, "what are you doing? Are you out of your senses to be accepting this man? Are you completely ignorant of his reputation?"

She endeavoured, with some confusion, to persuade her father of her attachment to Colonel Fitzwilliam. Her father seemed rather unconvinced. He had not been wholly unaware of her tendency to tag along with Darcy and Richard, whenever they visited the Matlock estate. To his thinking, it was just as it had been with her brother, Lord Harry, and his friends, ever since she first started to walk. She possessed all the elegance and charm of a princess, coupled with such athletic prowess any man might envy. Her preference for Darcy was clear; the only intimation she had ever shown that she might actually fancy a young gentleman. Darcy's seeming obliviousness of his daughter gave Lord Stafford a strong sense of comfort that nothing would ever become of her infatuation. Never in his wildest dreams would he have imagined that Richard might catch her eye. He voiced aloud, "They do not love that do not show their love."

The familiar refrain of his speech was not at all surprising. Her father was challenging her with the words of Shakespeare. It was he, who had fostered her love for the poet for as long as she could recall. Often, they were known to attempt to sway the opinion of the other, bantering about his words.

"Love goes by haps; some Cupid kills with arrows, some with traps," she responded, recalling the time of her first kiss with her betrothed. For what else was it, but a trap, a subterfuge on his part? Clearly, she did not intend that Richard should enter her apartment that night. No, Mr. Darcy knew exactly what he was about in passing on her note to his cousin, she often thought. She must thank him.

"It has always been the fondest wish of both your mother and me that you should marry a man you truly esteemed. Even whilst YOU insisted that you would only consider marriage to one whose fortune was suitable to your own. Colonel Fitzwilliam is amiable, to be sure, but he has no fortune of his own. He is merely a second son.

"And what of your long embraced stance on the matter of matrimony?" Lord Stafford asked. "Have I not often heard you preach—*hasty marriage seldom proveth well*? Nonetheless, you seem eager to rush into this union. Colonel Fitzwilliam says that it is your fervent wish to be married in under a month, by special license."

How earnestly did she then wish that her former opinions had been more reasonable, her expressions more moderate! "Love is begun by time, and time qualifies the spark and fire of it," she responded.

"Harriette, my dear," said her father, "I have given him my consent. I now give it to you, if you are resolved on having him. However, let me advise you to think better of it. I know your disposition, Harriette. I know you could be neither happy nor respectable, unless you truly esteemed your husband; unless you looked up to him as your superior. Your lively talents would place you in the greatest danger, in an unequal marriage. Let me not have the grief of seeing you unable to respect your partner in life. I beg of you, to know what you are about." Again, in Shakespeare's words he uttered, "This above all, to thine own self be true."

Deeply affected by her father's apprehension, she was earnest and solemn in her reply; and at length by repeated assurances that Colonel Fitzwilliam was really the object of her choice. She explained how he excited and challenged her like no one had ever done before, and how she truly esteemed him and adored him.

Persuaded, her father welcomed her into his caring embrace. His thoughts whispered, *love hath made thee a tame snake.*

~ ~ ~

Lady Catherine gasped in shock with the news of the engagement. Though, it was hardly noticed. The rest of the Fitzwilliam family was delighted. Lady Matlock said a silent prayer as she observed the look upon her son's face when he beheld his betrothed. Not only had he chosen someone of great fortune, he had chosen the beautiful daughter of one of her dearest friends,

Lady Stafford. The closest the two women had ever come to discussing a possible alliance (aside from the marriage of Georgiana and Lord Harry) was when they endeavoured to put young Harriette in Darcy's path. Darcy's marriage to Elizabeth cast all hopes for another marriage between the two distinguished families aside. Though, Lady Stafford would not admit it, she did not intend that her daughter should marry a second son. Any disappointment she felt in that regard, she did not share with her friend.

Lord Harry was pleased that his young sister was to be married to a man he had already come to know as an older brother, not only for Richard's original championing of his union with Georgiana but also because of the immense regard his dear wife held for her cousin. Georgiana herself smiled with delight even as she looked at her dearest friend and sister, Elizabeth, to gauge her reaction. One could only guess what the other was thinking.

Lady Catherine kept her eyes firmly trained upon her nephew and Lady Harriette throughout the evening. When at last the two parted company, she seized upon the young woman. Despite her size, she practically dragged the statuesque young beauty off to a quiet corner of the room.

"You might be able to fool my unsuspecting nephew with this little ruse, but you do not fool me one bit."

"Whatever do you mean, dear Aunt?" Lady Harriette asked sarcastically.

"Do not get ahead of yourself young woman. You are not married to my nephew just yet. If I have anything to say in the matter, this marriage shall never come to pass."

"Do not be ridiculous. He loves me, and I love him. There is nothing that you can do or say to change that."

"Just a month ago, you were hopelessly in love with Darcy," boasted Lady Catherine. "I am utterly convinced he visited you in your boudoir. Perhaps, you think that in marrying Fitzwilliam, you shall forever bind yourself to Darcy."

Lady Harriette looked at her own outstretched hand and admired the stunning engagement ring that Richard gave her. It was his paternal grandmother's ring; one that Lady Catherine believed should have been given to her upon her dear mother's passing. She bore the young woman a look that would surely cut right through the magnificent diamond stones.

Lady Harriette smirked. "Speaking of being hopeless, I do believe it is the one appellation that best describes you. Take my words of advice, mind your own business. Do not dare to try to cause trouble in my affairs. I assure you that you have nothing to gain, and everything to lose." At that moment, she looked about to see Richard and Darcy enter the room. Returning her attention to her Ladyship, she said, "I beg your pardon, dear Aunt. I see my *true* love has just returned."

She quickly crossed the room with the sole purpose of provoking her Ladyship. Rendering Lady Catherine utterly amazed, she approached both gentleman and enfolded her arms through either of theirs. She commenced a shameless flirtation with both men, all the while keeping one eye on Lady Catherine, until the elderly woman could take no more.

She soon stood and proceeded to leave the room in a huff. She could be heard uttering, "Why! I never saw such scandalous behaviour in my life!"

Lady Harriette's satisfaction with herself could not be contained. She fought mightily to stifle her laughter. Lady Catherine's precipitous exit did not go unnoticed by Richard. He excused himself from his cousin and led his incorrigible intended aside.

"What are you up to now, young lady?"

"What makes you think I am up to anything at all, other than enjoying the company of my beloved betrothed and his best friend in the world?"

"Pray tell me, you are not having fun at my aunt's expense."

"Well, now that you speak of it. She did mention her great suspicion that a certain *Fitzwilliam* visited me in my apartment."

"And did you say anything that might put her mind at ease?"

"What would you have me say?" Lady Harriette asked coyly.

"Let me think. Perhaps, you might have suggested that a certain *Fitzwilliam* shall be visiting you again—tonight."

"Heavens forbid! Why would I dare to speak such a scandalous falsehood?"

Richard leaned in close and whispered, "Scandalous, perhaps—but a falsehood, I think not."

Rendered speechless by his nearness, she found herself at quite a disadvantage. She would have loved to have him join her in her room, so she sensed. She relived their first encounter in her apartment, his skilful touch along her bosom, his lips upon hers, night after night. Despite her bravado, she was a mere maiden. And Richard had a way of affecting her sensibilities, such that she had never experienced. She could not explain it, except that it was the one time when he held a most decided advantage over her. The thought that he might visit her that night left her weak in the knees. By then, Richard stood directly behind her. The warmth of his breath upon the back of her long, slender neck sent her heart racing. *We are in a room full of family members. What is he thinking?*

"Harriette, may I come to you tonight?"

Her heart beat even faster. In silence, she screamed out a resounding, *YES!* The prospect of it all rendered her far more nervous than she would ever admit. She said nothing.

He allowed his fingers to trace the small of her back as he moved to stand especially close by her side. Taking her hand in his, he whispered in her ear, "I shall take your silence as yes; to-night." He raised her hand to his lips, but rather than kiss the back as would have been proper amidst a room full of people, he kissed the inside of her palm. She was powerless to protest as she felt an increasingly familiar wetness, when ever he behaved thus. Richard knew exactly the disarming effect he had on her. Though he could not wait to take her to their wedding bed, he felt strongly that he would. In the meantime, he meant to put a stop to her shameless flirtations with Darcy, as well as with himself—but especially with Darcy. After that night, he had no doubt that he would accomplish just that.

"Come, Lady Harriette. I believe it is your turn to exhibit on the pianoforte. I shall like nothing better than to turn the pages for you," he said as he took her arm in his before continuing in a hushed, sensuous tone, "for now."

From across the room, Lady Stafford observed the entire interlude. *That RAKE!* She gently smiled even as she considered the words. *A love match indeed..., I suspect my beautiful daughter has truly met her equal.*

~ ~ ~

The wedding of the only daughter of an earl, as well as the further joining of the two prominent families, was indeed a cause for celebration and one that found the Fitzwilliams, the Middletons, and the Darcys reunited once again within a month of their parting in Matlock.

With such an abbreviated courtship, such that it was, and an equally brief engagement, Richard prevailed and even managed to take Lady Harriette to their wedding bed hymen unchallenged, though barely.

Richard sat alone in the private dining room of the villa, quietly tapping his fingers whilst waiting for his tardy bride to join him. They had travelled to the continent for their honeymoon. It was the first they had been apart since the start of the wedding journey for any meaningful stretch of time. She insisted upon a morning of shopping in the fashionable district. He insisted he would have no part in it.

It delighted him to observe his wife to be as graceful and charming in ballroom settings as she was deft and agile on horseback, or as much as he was loathe admitting, in a fencing match. Indeed, she was quite the social butterfly. Fluent in several languages, she was as comfortable on the continent, as she was in any London elite society. He had come to know her as one of the most beautiful women he had ever beheld. He could not help but notice how other men thought so, as well. Greater than eleven years his wife's senior, he was beginning to feel it. Her power over him was immense, even as he endeavoured not to allow her to know it. The familiar calling of his given name every time he made her his, gave him to know that he had nothing to fear.

Richard's reverie was pleasantly halted when he espied his lovely wife at the door of their private dining-room. She was behaving charmingly coquettish whilst speaking with a handsome stranger. The man seemed none too comfortable upon spotting Richard, whom he recognised as her gentleman companion, even if he knew none of the particulars.

What is my lovely wife up to now? Richard arose from his seat and proceeded to the door to rescue the stranger. He could

178 P O Dixon

only smile; secure in the knowledge that surely he would never become bored.

~ *Chapter 15* ~
Always

Time enough had passed to witness the birth of the next generation of Darcys. The birth of Georgiana's son preceded that of the heir of Pemberley by three weeks. On the occasion of the latter child's reaching six months of age, the Middletons and the Fitzwilliams were all at Pemberley.

Lady Ellen sat comfortably in her deeply cushioned chair, gazing down upon the children as they slept. She found it impossible not to dote upon the two infants. She loved the two little angels, as if they were her own grandchildren, just as she loved Darcy and Georgiana as her own. She felt extremely blessed and even more so as she considered that both of her daughters were with child.

It was absolutely astounding, the transformation that Richard's marriage brought forth, not only in himself, but in his brother, Lord Robert, as well. Lord Matlock had played his hand in forcing his eldest son to be more of a husband to his wife and desist in his debauchery with his mistress in town, or risk the loss of a significant portion of his financial inheritance to Richard. It worked. Finally, Lord Robert had become the husband to Lady Elise that he ought, and after five years of marriage, they were starting their own family.

Richard and Lady Harriette settled at an estate that was bequeathed to him by Lady Ellen, upon his marriage. She delighted in the knowledge that they were settled near Matlock, for she would have all her grandchildren in proximity. Of course, this arrangement greatly benefited both Richard and Darcy, as well, as they maintained their close bond.

As Elizabeth sat in a relaxing chair on the terrace next to Lady Ellen, she could not help but reflect upon the dramatic changes in her life of the past few years. The life she enjoyed being so far removed from what she might have envisioned for herself. Darcy and she did not spend that past Season in town. That was one tradition they both gladly passed up. They were determined that their child would be born at Pemberley. For the first time in his adult life, Darcy did not spend Easter at Rosings Park. Though Darcy could say with absolute certitude that he did not miss his aunt's company that year, Elizabeth could not say the same of her own aunt.

It seemed Elizabeth was ever in the company of her husband's family, and never in the company of her own. Elizabeth's relations did not visit Pemberley at Christmas, as they had the year before. Elizabeth sought to remedy the absence of her loved ones with as many letters as her scheduled afforded. Her letters with Mrs. Gardiner were a godsend, as she eagerly sought her aunt's advice on the things an expectant mother would need to know and understand. Her aunt always replied just as eagerly.

Letters from Jane continued to speak of the many trials of raising two small children, running a household with a very few servants, and striving to live far below their means in a manner to which she truly had never wished to become accustomed. Something she would only share with Elizabeth was the admittedly foolish thoughts that pervaded her mind for months. Jane feared that she might be well on a path to living her mother's life; should her family be blessed with a baby girl. Such irrational concerns were put to rest with the birth of a bouncing baby boy.

Glad tidings abounded as Elizabeth received letters from her sisters Mary and Kitty, as well. Both gave birth to baby boys, within two months of the other. Mrs. Bennet was up to her neck in grandsons, so much so that she began to pray the next grandchild might be a little girl.

One of the many missives from her dear friend Grace shared the news of the birth of two beautiful twin daughters. Lady Grace wrote in a manner that scarcely concealed her ecstasy, for not only had her family grown at a faster pace than she had expected, but her sister Caroline had finally gotten her own establishment. A veritable blessing it turned out to be for everyone concerned; Caroline seemed not to have a maternal bone in her body. The prospect of being in the company of her infant nieces for anything beyond mere minutes at a time was more than she could bear.

Elizabeth missed her closest friends and family exceedingly. Not only did Darcy enjoy having his cousin Richard as a neighbour, but Elizabeth benefited from the arrangement, as well. Lady Harriette and she grew close to one another, and while they would never be as close as Elizabeth and Georgiana; the two got along swimmingly during their frequent visits at one another's homes. Indeed, it was Lady Harriette herself who remained by Elizabeth's side providing sisterly comfort and care during the birth of her child.

The entire Fitzwilliam family had gathered at Pemberley—everyone except Lady Catherine and Anne, that is. Poor Anne was bound to her vindictive mother, and as such was not able to take part in such family gatherings, despite her overwhelming desire to do so.

Lady Ellen thought it was a shame that Lady Catherine had chosen to isolate herself that way, rendering herself unable to be there to appreciate the blessings of the family, all because she could not dictate her nephew's life. She still had not accepted the marriage between Darcy and Elizabeth. Then again, Lady Ellen considered that Lady Catherine seemed none too accepting of Richard's marriage either. She did not have a single good thing to say of his lovely bride. She staunchly refused to attend the elaborate wedding ceremony. Lady Ellen could not help but wonder what that was all about.

Her Ladyship reflected upon the many changes in her life over the past two years. *Robert, Richard, and Fitzwilliam personify everything I could ever have wished them to be—happily settled, responsible, and loving husbands. I am so very proud of the men they have become.*

~ ~ ~

Some months earlier, Darcy felt himself on the outside looking in. Once again, he was attempting to persuade Elizabeth to attend to her other duties as mistress of Pemberley, beyond those of mother to their child. Though she shared his bed, she was always dressed in a nightgown. He knew it was acceptable for them to resume marital relations, having spoken with the doctor himself on the matter. By the time Elizabeth came to bed each night, she was far too exhausted for any amorous interludes. For more months than he cared to count, he had to mollify himself with chaste goodnight kisses and some incredibly painful cuddling where she tended to find herself nestled snugly within his embrace.

"If you would only consent to delegate more of the care of the baby to his army of nurses, you would have much more time for *me*." Darcy opined to his wife.

Elizabeth walked over to where her husband stood in the doorway of the room with her little bundle cradled in her arms. Elizabeth placed a kiss upon the baby's forehead. She raised her head. He leaned forward, and she kissed him upon his cheek, just as softly as she had kissed the child.

"See, there is enough room in my heart for both adorable Darcy men in my life."

An occasional peck on the cheek, hardly qualified as being a part of his wife's life, in his estimation. Elizabeth lavished so much attention on the baby. She did everything for him. She refused the convenience of a wet nurse, much to Darcy's dismay. Elizabeth was adamant that she would be the one responsible to provide the bulk of her son's care.

Elizabeth explained her strong stance to Darcy. "I will have little enough time with our son before he reaches an age where he will only want to tag along with you. I mean to enjoy every single moment that I now have with him. If I know you at all, you will have our son on horseback by the time he takes his first step. He will be off to Eton before he can spell his full name."

"Elizabeth, I do not wish to deprive you of this time with our son, but you do have other responsibilities, and I am not speaking of the management of the household."

"What exactly are you speaking of, Mr. Darcy?"

"You know of what I speak, Mrs. Darcy."

"What I know is that I desire more than anything in the world that my son should always know what he means to me." She went on to explain that she knew her mother must have loved her in her own way, but sometimes she had her doubts. She never wanted her son or any of the other children she hoped to have, to feel that way, ever.

Darcy reminded her that he needed her too. "Not that I consider the baby a competitor for your attention, of course he needs you the most, but it is your own decision to take everything upon yourself. It does not seem fair. What about me?"

"Fair! I do not believe you at times. You are as self-centred as ever," she calmly reproached, without directing her focus away from her son. He had fallen asleep in her arms.

"If it is self-centred to wish to be intimate with my wife once again, then I am guilty as charged."

Elizabeth placed the sleeping child in his cradle. After looking upon him lovingly for one last time before directing her full attention to her husband, she said, "I suppose I might speak with the doctor, to hear what he recommends on the matter."

"I have done that already. He informs me that there is no cause for concern."

"William, I suppose I should be infuriated with you for your presumption, but I will endeavour not to be. I too miss our intimacy."

"Truly?" He placed his hands lovingly about her waist, drew her closer, and kissed her softly. "What say you to this moment? He is asleep after all."

"Yes, this is the time for his nap, which gives me a brief amount of time to meet with Mrs. Reynolds and tend to other matters. Tonight, I promise."

Darcy was happy with anything he could get at that point. He had her promise—that night it would be.

Unfortunately, for Darcy, when the night-time came, one thing led to another with the baby requiring every bit of her attention. Elizabeth actually fell asleep in the midst of Darcy's attempts to ready her for a night of passion.

Darcy was forced to recall an earlier disagreement that he had with Elizabeth a month or so before the baby was born. He learnt from Mrs. Reynolds that Elizabeth had made no effort to hire a wet-nurse and a nursery maid for their unborn child.

Thinking that she was too busy to handle the matter, he took the task of arranging it upon himself.

Darcy introduced the newly hired staff members to her as a matter that had been quite decided and not subject to change. Elizabeth was not at all pleased. She could hardly wait until the two of them were alone.

"There is no need to thank me."

"I should say not."

"What is it now?"

"You made this decision without consulting me!"

"Indeed, I saw what needed to be done, and I did it. Am I to consult you on every decision that I make, Mrs. Darcy?"

"As regards household matters and specifically the care of our child, I insist upon it."

"I fail to see the problem. Our child will need both a wet-nurse and a nursery maid. You did not seem inclined to address these concerns any time soon. There was no need to put it off any longer."

"I have put if off because I mean to attend to all my child's needs, personally."

"Elizabeth, you cannot be serious." Darcy thought but did not voice aloud, *the mistress of Pemberley attending to her own child, nursing her own child. What on earth is she thinking?*

"Indeed, I am quite serious."

To his continuing dismay, she remained true to her words. Elizabeth refused to avail herself to many of the services that her staff members were there to provide. Hardly anything was done for the infant, that she did not do herself.

A few nights subsequent to the thwarted attempt at romance, after what had been a particularly long day, she made slow progress into bed, cuddled up in Darcy's arms and immediately fell into a deep, exhausted sleep. Between the baby, her duties as mistress and hence some unexpected tenant responsibilities, she was worn out. She did not even stir as the baby cried in the adjoining room. Elizabeth had converted part of her suite into a makeshift nursery so that she could be close to her son during the night. The alternative would have been to bring a cradle into the master's suite. Darcy did not take to that idea at all.

Darcy tried to rouse her but eventually abandoned his attempts. He put on his robe and went to tend to the child himself.

He had never been alone with the baby before. He was quite nervous and uncertain about what to do. Frantically, he recalled his wife's instructions on how to hold the infant. Seeing how the little fellow would not stop crying, and Elizabeth did not come, he had no choice but to put his scant knowledge to use.

Once securely cradled in his arms, Darcy spoke to the baby as he would have an adult.

"Are you going to stop crying? Are you hungry? Did your mother not feed you just hours ago?" To his surprise, his voice seemed a soothing melody; the more he spoke, the calmer the baby became.

Darcy's astonishment could scarcely be described. He looked at the precious child in his arms and his heart melted. The beautiful bundle was not just the fulfilment of his legacy—the heir to Pemberley. He held his own son, a truly wondrous and precious life—the fruit of his love for Elizabeth. Darcy sat down and studied his child's face. He was awestruck. It astounded him what the miraculous little wonder meant to him.

How could I fault my wife for devoting herself to him? How could I have felt even a tinge of jealousy? If Elizabeth told me that she loved our child more than anything else in the world, I would well understand what she meant.

As he pondered all that he would do to cherish and protect his son in the days, months, and years to come, he came to appreciate his wife's seemingly boundless devotion.

Some time later, Elizabeth woke with a start!

It was after dawn. She sensed she had slept for hours. She panicked as her immediate thoughts were of her child. She wondered how her son was doing. She had no awareness if he had awakened during the night. Elizabeth quickly donned her robe and headed for her suite. She hoped that, at the very least, his nurse might have attended to his needs.

She felt guilty. She considered that perhaps she had gotten it all wrong. She could not do it all. It was time that she availed herself to extra help. It seemed the longest few yards she had ever walked.

Elizabeth went to the baby's cradle only to find it empty. She nearly fainted. Just then, she turned to see her husband reclined on his back, with their son resting contentedly on his chest. She slowly crept forward to witness the most divine sight imaginable. Two beautiful Darcy males slept peacefully, the countenance of the eldest as tranquil and innocent as that of the youngest.

After pausing, for a few moments, to admire her two greatest loves, she decided it was time to stir their son for his morning feeding. Sensing Elizabeth's efforts, Darcy awakened. He opened his eyes to the breathtaking image he had studied intently for the last half hour before succumbing to sleep—his son's resemblance in his beloved wife's face.

Wishing not to disturb the precious child, he whispered softly, "Please, do not take him away just yet. I wish to stay here with our son a while longer."

"If that is your wish. Is there room enough in your arms for your wife?"

"Always, my love," Darcy whispered as he made room and received Elizabeth into his warm embrace. He kissed her lovingly upon her forehead, "Always."

Do not miss the beginning of this engaging and provocative adaptation of
Jane Austen's

Pride and Prejudice

Mr. Darcy's Tale

Available online and where books are sold

PODixon.com

<u>Acknowledgements and Credits</u>

Jane Austen's *"Pride and Prejudice"*

William Shakespeare's
"Henry VI"
"Much Ado About Nothing"
"As You Like It"
"Midsummer Night's Dream"
"Twelfth Night"
"The Two Gentlemen from Verona"
"Hamlet"

The JAFF Community

William Shakespeare's Famous Quotes referenced in this book

She's beautiful, and therefore, to be woo'd
She is woman, therefore, to be won
Henry VI Part I - Act V

They do not love that do not show their love
The Two Gentlemen of Verona ~ Act I

Love goes by haps; some Cupid kills with arrows, some
with traps
Much Ado About Nothing ~ Act III

Hasty marriage seldom proveth well
Henry VI Part III - Act IV

This above all, to thine own self be true
Hamlet - Act I

Love hath made thee a tame snake
As You Like It ~ Act IV

Other quotes that might also apply to Colonel Fitzwilliam and Lady Harriette's improbable love...

The course of true love never did run smooth
Midsummer Night's Dream ~ Act I

Love sought is good, but given unsought is better
Twelfth Night ~ Act III

If music be the food of love, play on
Twelfth Night ~ Act I

Love looks not with eyes, but with the mind
Midsummer Night's Dream ~ Act I

Can you think of others?

CPSIA information can be obtained at www.ICGtesting.com
Printed in the USA
241149LV00001B/4/P